SAN FRANCISCO

Also by Terence Clarke

Novels
My Father in The Night
The King of Rumah Nadai
A Kiss for Señor Guevara
The Notorious Dream of Jesús Lázaro
The Splendid City (English language)
La espléndida ciudad (Spanish language)
When Clara Was Twelve
The Moment Before

Story collections
The Day Nothing Happened
Little Bridget and The Flames of Hell
New York

Non-fiction
Fathers, Sons, and Seizures
The Sea Lion and The Sculptor
An Arena of Truth: Conflict in Black and White

SAN FRANCISCO

STORIES BY

TERENCE CLARKE

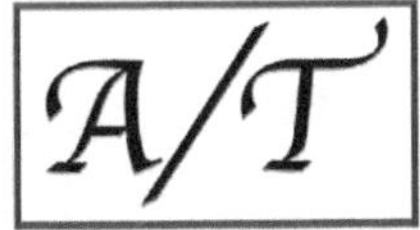

For Beatrice Bowles
Querida narradora

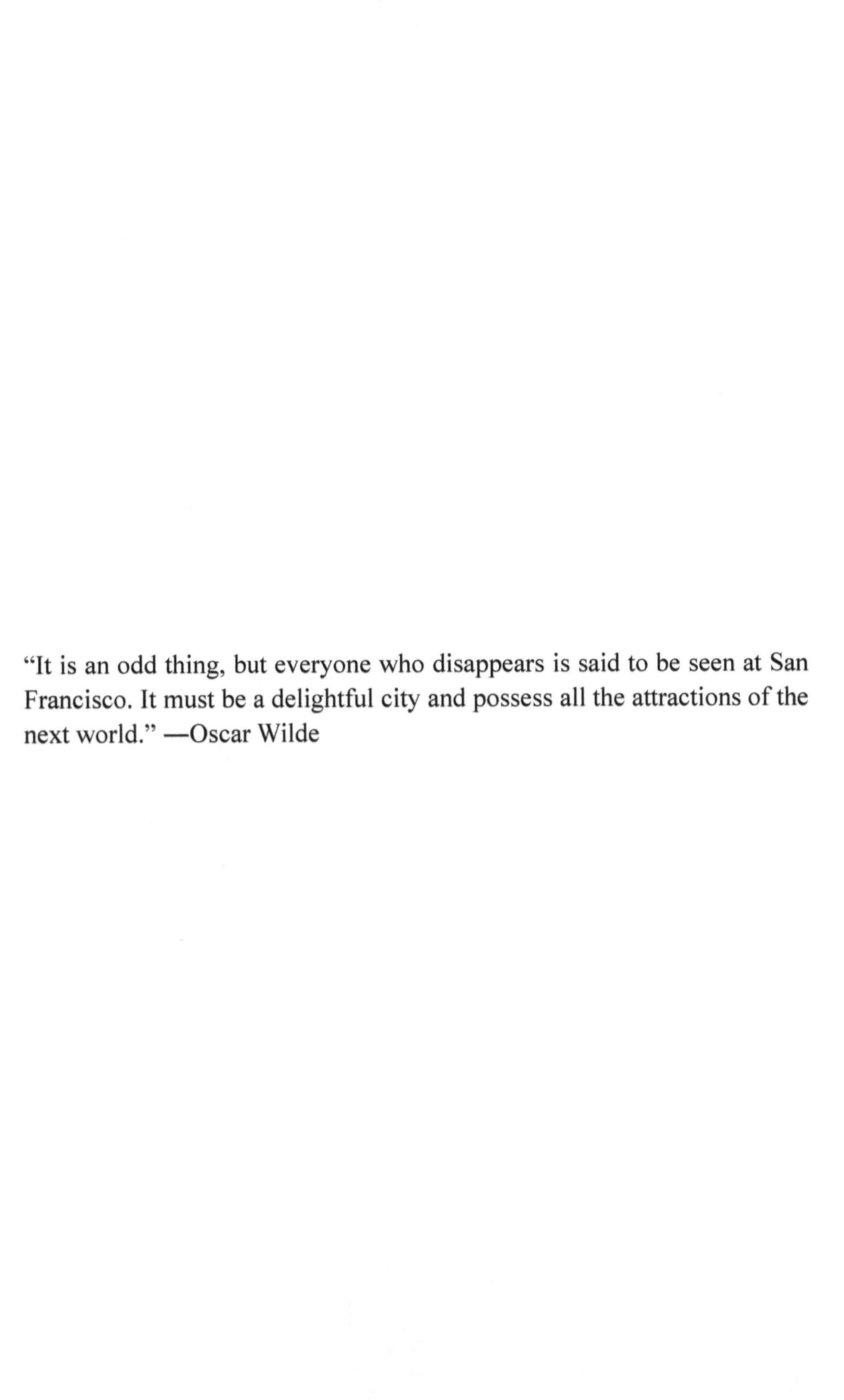

"It is an odd thing, but everyone who disappears is said to be seen at San Francisco. It must be a delightful city and possess all the attractions of the next world." —Oscar Wilde

CONTENTS

EUGENE LI AND THE QUEEN OF ENGLAND

Eugene got the call to go rescue Lizzie. He was in front of the Vallejo Street station house enjoying the morning sun when Ismael came out to get him.

"Where?"

"Chinatown. They need somebody down there who can do the Cantonese."

Eugene sighed. He was the officer of choice to look into most things in Chinatown because, although there were a couple other Chinese guys in the station who could well do the Cantonese, he was the only one who had actually been born in Guangdong…in the city of Guangzhou, to be precise.

The people in Chinatown recognized this. Eugene was young. Yes, he was a fluent English-speaking American. But because of his own beginnings—and due to his friendship with younger cousins who had arrived in the U.S. more recently—he also had the coolest Cantonese slang. Others whose antecedents had come across a generation or two before did not have Eugene's hip fluency. Their slang was from the Eighties or Nineties, and they were therefore identified right away as uncool.

"You don't sound like my grandfather," a young waiter at Hunan Home's on Jackson Street had said to him just this morning. A newly arrived Stockton Street butcher with no English at all was amazed to hear Eugene speak so fluently with all the latest intonations and fun. A cute Grant Avenue nail polish girl flirted with him because he could talk with her with such humorous ease. They liked Eugene. Eugene *was* cool…and, to be sure, his English was cool too. In that language, he didn't have the oafish, know-it-all intonations of the white officers in the station. When he was busting a white teenage skateboarder for reckless speeding the wrong way down Grant Avenue while making the finger at the tourists, Eugene could give the kid the appropriate insistent order in English that the kid could not mistake.

Eugene was also handsome, an object of interest for many of the younger women shopping or working on Stockton Street. He kept to himself, although not from shyness. He felt that he could possibly jeopardize any girl from the neighborhood who might be seen going out with him. There *is* crime in Chinatown, mostly related to drugs and gang dealings. Those offenses are the domain of police inspectors and such…guys higher up the department food chain than Eugene himself. But were one of the shopgirls to be seen stepping out with Eugene, she could possibly be targeted by someone unscrupulous, and Eugene did not want to be responsible for such a threat to an innocent.

Walking with Ismael on Columbus Avenue a few days ago, he had suggested coffee at Caffé Greco, a place both policemen liked. Ismael was a fan of the tiramisu here and, besides, his cousin Elias worked behind the counter. A Guatemalan, Elias was illegal. Eugene knew that. But Ismael was a legal citizen, born in Los Banos, California. So, Ismael and Eugene both did what they could to advise Elias how to stay off the Homeland Security radar.

"Look, I've got to say hello to Father Serra," Ismael said to Eugene. "At Peter and Paul." The church was just a few blocks away. Eugene knew that Ismael went to Confession there, whatever that was, and that the cop and the priest were friends. "I'll be along in a couple minutes. Get me a cappuccino, will you, and a tiramisu?"

The café had just two other customers, an elderly white man and a young white girl. A copy of *Fodor's San Francisco* rested open on the man's table, and at the counter Elias was advising the girl about the café's pastries. Her head was lowered toward the glass case that held them, and she was holding an index finger to her lips. There is ice cream in a second case, but Eugene could tell right away that she was not considering it. Elias, attentive and delighted, was taking her through all the pastries.

Eugene nodded to the man who, smiling, waved a hand at him. "H'lo, Constable." An Irish accent. "Mind a question?"

Eugene approached his table.

"You're Chinese, I believe."

Eugene chortled. "How'd you guess?"

Chastened, the man shrugged. "Well…." He glanced toward his cup of tea. "You know…."

"Right. My name's Eugene. What can I do to help you?"

"I'd like a bit of advice. Chinatown's right here, isn't it?" He pointed to the guidebook.

"Sure. Up the block there and turn left. That's Stockton Street. Chinatown goes on from there for blocks."

"But is it safe in Chinatown?" The Irishman looked about. "I was watchin' a documentary last night at the hotel…you know, it was about Chinatown, and there were masses of people in it. Every sidewalk crowded. Noise everywhere. You know…talk, talk, and talk."

"That's the way we are."

"Well…is it safe?"

"Safe!"

"Ay. Can you walk there?"

"Uh, Mr.…Mr…?"

"Daly. Callum Daly." Callum pointed to the girl, who apparently had made her choice. "We won't be attacked, will we?"

Eugene rumbled to himself. "In Chinatown?"

"Yeh."

Eugene motioned toward a chair and sat down at the table. Taking a moment to get Elias's attention, he held up two fingers. Elias understood the order right away and nodded.

Eugene folded his hands and leaned forward. "Look, Mr. Daly, I've made three arrests on Stockton Street since I've been with the force, and that's in three years."

"Just three?"

"I've made other arrests, of course, a lot of them, but in other neighborhoods. Just three here."

"What were they for, then?"

"One for shoplifting, another when a guy making an illegal turn a few blocks from here had blocked another guy from continuing on straight. He insulted the other guy, and they had a fistfight in the intersection."

"The third?"

"A homeless guy walking down the middle of Stockton Street without any pants on."

"Any underpants?"

"No."

Callum smiled. "All of them Chinese, I suppose."

"Nope. All white boys."

"Really?"

"All white. And one of them…the guy making the wrong turn…you know, scraggly hair, Oakland Raiders shirt…he called me a chink as I was escorting him to a holding cell." Eugene now smiled, and Callum could tell that the policeman was about to share a pleasantry. "I sort of helped him into the holding cell, you might say." He made an abrupt, short-fused gesture with both hands before him.

Laughing, Callum gestured toward the front counter. "That's my granddaughter Lizzie over there."

"She's Irish, too."

"All her life, mate. Just like me."

"The same accent."

"The same. Although…" Callum looked toward the girl, who was still in conversation with Elias. "I've heard her utterin' words I've never heard, or don't understand."

"Regular English words?"

"Slang." Callum grinned. "Kids' talk!" He surveyed the open palms of his hands. "The Brits are famous for it, you know." He nodded. "Shakespeare and that lot." He laid a hand on his chest. "And look what you Americans have done to the poor language." Responding to Eugene's smile, Callum shrugged. "Well, the lads in Dublin are pretty good at it, too." He frowned in a way that made Eugene laugh. "But now, we're too old for Lizzie and her girlfriends. They understand us, but we don't understand them." Callum's grin grew. He nodded toward the girl, who was returning to the table with a single plate on which was a large piece of marbled chocolate cake, heavy with frosting.

"What is it you have there, love?"

"He told me it was the best," Lizzie said. The plate had two forks on it. "He said you'd like it."

"I expect I will." Callum pulled the third chair from the table and gestured to it. "This is Garda Eugene."

"H'lo," Lizzie was about twelve. She wore a pair of gym tights…green, yellow, and red swirls…a turtleneck T-shirt, and a dark blue hoodie on which was printed the face of a full-throated James Brown. Her purple Doc Martens were quite badly scuffed, their white laces new and bright.

"Or would it be 'officer?' Officer Eugene?" Callum said.

"Just 'Eugene,'" Eugene said.

Lizzie sat down.

"You're a James Brown fan, Lizzie?" Eugene folded his hands on the table. "So, uh…how do you feel?"

Her hair was cut short, almost a crewcut around the sides, straight and much longer on top, all of it dyed jet-black, with one single blonde stripe down the middle from front to back. She also wore a single earring, a slim brass circle that formed a kind of pale around her right cheek.

She glanced at Eugene, fingering the edge of the plate. Suddenly she gave him an innocence-emblazoned smile. "I feel good!"

They both laughed, and Eugene could tell, from Callum's seeming confusion, that the older man had not gotten the reference.

"But how do you know about James Brown? I mean, he died years ago."

"All the kids love his stuff," she said. "He makes you dance. Wilson Pickett, too. The Supremes."

"But what about the people singing now."

"Like who?"

"Oh…Rico Nasty?"

"So cool."

"Amy Winehouse?"

Lizzie was too busy for further conversation. Her eyes were fixed on the cake.

"So dead," she whispered.

He himself understood the passion that was enveloping her just in this moment. His own great-grandfather, Li Yeun, who had come to the U.S. as a young man, made money as a fish monger and then with real estate, and never learned a word of English, had himself loved chocolate cake, introduced to it by Eugene at Victoria Pastry on Stockton Street when Eugene was eight.

"This is chocolate," Yeun had said. He examined the piece of cake as though it were a mind-thwarting puzzle…each turn of frosting, every crumb that had strayed onto the plate, even the thick line of frosting between the two layers of cake. He prodded it here and there with his fork, as though he suspected something poisonous.

"Yeah." Eugene's use of the English word did not phase his great-grandfather, who, convinced by the little boy (whom Li Yeun greatly enjoyed and whose parents he had been able to bring to the U.S. with the two year-old Eugene in tow), plunged the fork into the cake, tasted it, and then quite hurriedly took another, larger forkful.

"I read the Chinese own a good deal of San Francisco," Callum said.

"Some of it."

"A lot of it, I read."

A slight grumbling surged through Eugene, a sadness that he had felt often as he had grown up. He had known he was far more cool than most of the white boys in his schools, who were surly and uncommunicative, especially with the Chinese kids. Eugene felt he was a lot smarter than those white boys, too. He took after his great-grandfather who, though he could not speak English, had a kind of warm, home-grown emotional sense and real practicality that Eugene had always paid attention to, even when he himself had been a surly teenager.

Elias arrived with two cappuccinos, two tiramisus, and two forks.

"I'll tell you a story," Eugene said.

He sipped from his coffee. Lizzie, involved with her cake, seemed not to be listening.

"My great-grandfather bought buildings where he could," Eugene said.

"In San Francisco," Callum said.

"Yes. At first below Chinatown, along Kearney Street down there, when they were just rundown warehouses, old office buildings. Shops and things. Up the hill, too. The lower part of Russian Hill…" He took more coffee. "Mason Street and below. Not above Mason Street."

"So, he was part of the great American story, eh?"

"The story."

"Yes…. I mean no offense, but you Yanks do like to brag about your thrivin' democracy…. Anyone can make it here. Pullin' yourself up by your bootstraps. All that."

"Maybe so," Eugene muttered before speaking up again. "But there's more to our great democracy than that."

"How so?"

"My great-grandfather could buy those buildings, but he couldn't live in them."

"Where *could* he live?"

Eugene leaned toward the café window and gestured toward Stockton Street. "There."

"Chinatown."

"*Only* in Chinatown."

Lizzie had started listening to the story. She held the chocolate-stained fork in her right hand, empty of any cake itself.

"I expect that changed with others who came later, though," Callum said.

"My parents?"

"Yes. What about them?"

Eugene shrugged. He placed the fingers of both hands around the mug of coffee and studied it a moment. He did not answer.

"Not your mum and da, too!" Lizzie said.

Eugene tightened his lips. "It was better for them. But it wasn't good."

"How could they do that?" Lizzie asked.

"Who?"

"The other lot that lived here."

"The white people, you mean."

"Yeh."

Eugene took up his own fork. He glanced at the slice of cake and then at Lizzie, his eyes making the obvious inquiry. She looked at the cake herself and then pushed the plate toward Eugene.

"They had the law on their side," he said as he nudged a piece of frosting onto the fork.

"You mean…." Lizzie pointed to Eugene's badge. "You?"

"No, Lizzie." He pushed his tiramisu toward Lizzie and gestured to her to take some. She did, and, surprised by it, savored it, although she remained listening. Eugene looked down at his chest, at the dark blue shirt, the badge, the body camera, the radio, and further down, the handgun, the duty belt, the hand cuffs. "Not me."

"So even you can't live anywhere except in Chinatown?" Lizzie's lips were pressed together and skewed.

"Now I can, yes. But we had to sue them to make that possible."

"Sue them?" Callum said.

"Sometimes all the way up to the Supreme Court."

Lizzie placed the fork on her plate. "Where you won?" She folded her hands together.

"We did. But we still couldn't live just anywhere. So sometimes we had to go *back* to court."

Callum nodded. "So that you could—"

"Sue them again."

"Well done!" Callum folded his arms before him and glanced toward Lizzie, raising his eyebrows. "What would we call people like those eejits above…" He looked toward Eugene. "Which street?"

"Mason Street."

Lizzie frowned. The disapproval of what she had just heard from Eugene—her anger with the legal drudgery through which Eugene's family and all the other Chinese had had to go—seemed to come from a more mature, more knowledgeable consciousness than that of a twelve-year-old, and Eugene enjoyed the perturbed, understanding look on her face.

"I'd call them 'not nice,'" she said.

Callum nodded. "That's the least of it." He took another sip from his coffee. "You know, we had a little o' that ourselves in Ireland." He nodded to his granddaughter. "Lizzie knows about it."

Lizzie frowned and shook her head. "Yeh. Granda talks about this a lot."

Eugene sat back, waiting.

"He's gonna bring up the Brits now." Eugene sensed that this last from Lizzie was a bored throwaway. But the way she looked at Callum once she made the utterance betrayed the loving humor that she felt for him. "The post office siege, Granda? Bloody Sunday?"

"That's right, love. And wouldn't you bring those things up, too, if you had the chance? Croke Park. *All* that."

Eugene lifted a small glop of tiramisu onto his fork and brought it toward his mouth. "And we won those other cases too." He slipped the fork into his mouth.

"Good lad!" Callum sat back and looked out the window, folding his arms. He was pleased.

But now, a few days later, Lizzie was in some sort of trouble.

Ismael shielded his face from the sunlight and frowned. Forty-one years old, he had two daughters himself, both in high school in Oakland. He was a few pounds overweight and balding, and frequently kidded Eugene for his slim good looks. "Elias called me. He told me that that Irishman you introduced me to the other day just came into the Greco again. He's terrified, Elias says."

"What happened?

"He says his granddaughter's been taken."

"Where?"

Ismael clearly was worried for Lizzie. His mouth was tight. "Chinatown."

Eugene lowered his head. "Chinatown." With this whisper, he put his hands into his pants pockets.

"Elias was pretty confused when I talked to him," Ismael said. "He said he could barely understand what the Irish guy was saying, he was talking so fast. And, you know, that accent."

"Yeah."

"I've heard it before. You know, those immigrant guys…. The furniture movers. The house painters. Irish! Never makes any sense to me."

"I've heard that it sometimes doesn't make sense even to them," Eugene said.

"Well…." Ismael looked into Eugene's eyes. "I'll never know." Eugene could tell he was alarmed. "But those two are nice people."

"They are." Eugene looked himself over, to make sure he had all the usual equipment. "I'll go to the Greco now and talk to him."

Callum sat at a round table next to the large window that looks out from the Greco onto Columbus Avenue. He hailed Eugene as the policeman approached the doorway into the cafe.

At the table, Eugene saw how upset Callum really was. He was dressed in the same sport coat and slacks he had been wearing the other day. His blue dress shirt was now wrinkled and had a still-damp splotch of coffee just below the open collar. It was the result of a hurried, nervous slurp, Eugene surmised, taken too quickly.

"Eugene." Callum's skin seemed to sag even more than it had the other day. The youthfulness he had exhibited with Eugene's further description, of how it had been Chinese lawyers who had won all the Supreme Court decisions, had disappeared. Now there was stricken distress, even despair. Eugene had expected this…the quality of the old man's worry for his granddaughter. Callum's hands firmly clenched the mug of coffee. They were thick-fingered, one of them clearly recently chewed upon. His eyes seemed to burrow into the coffee itself, still steaming in the mug.

"What happened?"

"We went to the post office down Stockton Street there, the one you told us about. Lizzie had postcards…." Callum exhaled, his lips pressed together as he continued examining his hands and the mug. "She loves postcards, that little one." He fingered the edge of the table. "She had a couple dozen. You know, school chums, cousins—"

"Her parents."

Callum sighed. "Well, her mother, yes. My daughter. We don't know where her father is." He swallowed, a movement in his throat that appeared difficult, as though it were an utterance that simply could not be made in public. "Gobshite gombeen bank officer." He shrugged. He was disappointed with himself despite the fury of his remark. "Sorry, Eugene. It's just that he left Mary and Lizzie behind." His shoulders slumped once more. "Never a word from him. And not a Euro." Callum's eyes softened as he caressed the mug. "As far as we know, he's in Australia!" He stared down into it. "Those poor people. And that's where I stepped in, you see. You know, for Lizzie."

Callum slumped in his chair.

"So, what happened this morning?" Eugene said.

"She'd posted her cards, and I was next in the queue. She went outside, and told me she'd wait."

"She was gone when you got out there?"

"No. But she was almost gone. Some guy had forced her into his car."

"Forced her."

"That's right. And if you knew Lizzie the way I do, you'd realize she was makin' her own effort to bloody that eejit."

"But—"

"No. He was too big. One of those guys that, when he bends over like this one was, the crack in his arse is showin'. A baseball cap. Run-down shoes." Callum's lower lip disappeared into his mouth, and reappeared, glistening. "The baseball cap was on backwards." He exhaled.

"And they got away before you could get to them."

"They did. Lizzie was in the back seat. She could turn, and I saw that she'd spotted me. She jammed the palm of a hand against the rear wind screen, and she was yellin'."

"But they were gone."

"Lord help me, yes."

"Which direction."

"Into that tunnel."

Eugene fingered the cellphone. He had forgotten one important detail. "Chinese?"

"No! These were…what did you call them the other day? White boys." He shrugged, and it seemed to Eugene that the old man had suddenly gotten a good deal older. He looked at the tabletop as though it were an empty plain that somehow revealed Callum's guilt for not keeping a proper eye on his only grandchild.

"Were?"

"Yeh. Two of 'em. Your Yank white boys."

Eugene called Ismael about what had happened. He wanted to go to the post office and ask around in the shops on that block of Stockton Street, if they had seen anything. Ismael told him to go for it, and he'd let Lieutenant Spivey in the station know what had happened. "If he's got a problem with that, I'll call you. But keep us posted, Eugene, okay?"

Eugene told Callum to remain in the café. "I'll be back in an hour or two. So, don't go anywhere, eh?"

Callum nodded. "Good man."

"Give me your cellphone number."

Callum reached into his jacket pocket for a pen. He pulled a paper napkin up close.

"We'll find her." Eugene jammed the napkin into a pants pocket.

He went back to the station and requisitioned a car.

Molly Chin was the postal clerk. About fifty, her daughter Rose Anne had been in the same junior high school class as Eugene at Marina Middle School, and also at Galileo High. Eugene had played the glockenspiel in the high school band. He liked the instrument because you could hear it tinkling even when the crowd was screaming after a touchdown or something. Rose Anne had been stuck with a trumpet, which she played quite badly. She was just now in post-doctoral studies at Harvard.

"No, I didn't see anything, Eugene," Molly said. "Her grandfather was shaking when he came back in here. So, when he told me what had happened, I called the station, and Officer Ismael took the information."

"He told me."

"But I was inside here. I couldn't tell Ismael anything about it, except that it happened."

Eugene went out to the corner before the post office. Several people were gathered there, awaiting the traffic signal, and he shouted out, had anyone seen a white girl being taken away?. The talk among the people, the surprised, even aghast, reaction to the question, was a torrent of Cantonese. But no one had seen what had happened.

Eugene crossed the street, to Apple Land Vegetables and Fruit. The owner, Stanton Hui, nodded while arranging a display of durian, carefully, so as to avoid being poked by the sharp surfaces of the fruit's skin.

"I did see…" Stanton's voice fell to an exhaled breath. He pointed out to the sidewalk. "The big guy was pushing her into the car."

'What make?"

"I'm not sure. A Ford, I think. Four-door. Old. Ten years old, maybe. Blue. I thought she was just one of those teenage girls telling her father to leave her alone." He smiled, although with rueful acknowledgement now of what had actually taken place. "You see that sometimes with the whites." The suggestiveness with which he pronounced these last words in Cantonese revealed that Stanton had studied the whites who came into his store, almost always asking for directions to a good Chinese restaurant.

One of Stanton's customers, an elderly Chinese woman, the grey of whose hair was that of gunmetal, approached the two men. "I saw them." The hair was short, straight, and perfectly combed. She wore a black windbreaker and gray slacks, with tennis shoes, and was accompanied by an empty two-wheeled grocery cart. "There was another man at the wheel."

"Also white?" Eugene asked.

"Of course. He had a beard and sunglasses. But really, I couldn't tell you anything more about him. They were gone so quickly." Eugene noted the clarity of her accent in Cantonese. She was educated.

"When did you get here?" he asked.

"Ah! That!" She shook her head. "The Great Leap Forward."

"That long ago! And your parents, too?"

"I was twenty-five. A university student."

"But…your parents?"

The woman put a hand to her chest and looked down. "He was a university professor."

"They came with you?"

She remained silent, so long that Eugene surmised what her answer would be.

"They were killed."

Eugene acquiesced in his questioning. "Excuse me," he said. "I didn't mean to—"

"Oh, no, Officer." She had changed to English. "Those were terrible times. It's important we remember them." She turned toward Stanton. "We mustn't let that happen again, eh?"

"That's right," Stanton said.

She took the handle of her cart. "Please find that little girl."

"We will. I'll keep Stanton informed."

"Yes," the woman said. "Please do."

Eugene went through the tunnel and circled downtown for half an hour. He then returned to the Stockton Street post office and started a search up and down the streets of Chinatown. Nothing showed up. No blue Ford. No big guy. No Lizzie.

He widened the search and eventually arrived at the Marina Green. Its expansive view of the entry to the bay and the Golden Gate bridge gave up nothing except its usual heart-swirling beauty. A large flight of pelicans (one of Eugene's favorite birds to watch when he was a child walking out here with his great grandfather) in an enormous V-shaped formation, floated toward the bridge. The work they had to do to keep aloft was made obvious by the beating of their wings…as always, for Eugene, hurried industry in the service of serenity. Circling through the parking lots that line the green, Eugene saw no such car as Stanton had described. He did not know what to do. Where were they? They could be miles away, doing who-could-imagine-what to Lizzie, leaving her somewhere to suffer…*whatever*, Eugene anguished…with no help from anyone.

His phone buzzed. It was a message from Ismael. "Lizzie's granddad called us. He got a message from her on his phone. 'Help me,' it said. 'Fort Mason,' it said."

"Okay. I'm goin' there."

Fort Mason was quiet, a one-time army facility that now houses non-profits and serves as a kind of vernal, tourist walking attraction. From its central cliff overlooking the bay, it offers miraculous views of the water, sky, and bird life in every direction. Vista is its stunning gift.

Eugene drove up past the chapel building and the public vegetable garden to the hostel that commands the top of the slope overlooking the bay. He came here often on a break or to enjoy a coffee in a few moments by himself. Just now he had to calm himself because of his past-proven knowledge of what kidnappers of little girls do. He remained in the car looking out on the bay. A large empty field stretched between Eugene and the edge of the cliff that looks down on the now ramshackle docks that served the fort during World War II. A paved road runs along the edge of the cliff, sheltered by pine trees. Beyond the docks below, the bay itself forms the moving expanse—tide flowing in, waters lumbering out—that feeds the Pacific Ocean, and then is fed by it, back and forth. Eugene frequently tried to imagine what those tides carried…their immense fishery, the water itself tumbling down from the faraway sierra in the east, the whole millennias-old story transported by their slow comings and goings.

Lizzie, he thought. *Please. Where is she?*

He spotted her on one of the wood benches at the far end of the field. She was seated between two men who seemed to be arguing with each other. Viewed from behind, Lizzie's shoulders slumped, and Eugene could see that she was holding her hands to her face, as though wishing to silence the abrupt blurts of speech that surrounded her. Now and then, she shouted at the men.

He opened the car door and began sprinting across the field. One of the men saw him, and they ran from the bench toward the roadway. A long cement stairway leads down the cliff to the docks, and the men ran down it as Eugene arrived at the bench.

"I've got you, Lizzie." He took her into his arms. "I've got you. Don't worry."

At first terrified, she quickly realized that this was Eugene, and she put her arms around him, hiding her face against the front of his shirt. He forgot about the two white boys and determined to stay with the girl.

"It's all right. You're okay."

He looked over his shoulder, into the parking lot at the bottom of the stairs. The two men ran to an old blue sedan, which quickly scurried from its parking place. Smoke from its reeling tires floated behind as it sped toward the exit on Marina Boulevard.

Lizzie pulled away from Eugene. She glared at him. Taking up her backpack, she stepped away from the bench, her back a kind of blank accusation.

"Lizzie! It's me!"

She stumbled and halted. Bent over a moment, she looked back and, fear-drenched tears hurrying across her right hand, her backpack falling to the ground, she sat down on another bench and began openly weeping. Eugene stood and approached her. To his surprise, she glared at him as though *he* were the kidnapper.

"I thought you'd never find me!"

"Well, it took some time. I had to—"

"Where've you been?"

"All over the place. You know, your granddad, the post office, Chinatown, all over North Beach."

"Were any of your other gardas lookin' for me?" With this, Lizzie's cheeks and eyes tightened. She thrust her hands into the pockets of her hoodie and surveyed the toes of her Doc Martens. The right heel dug at a recess of dirt and a few of the needles that had dropped from one of the pines overhead. "You took your time, didn't ya?"

"Lizzie."

"You did, didn't ya? 'Who cares about Lizzie?,' that's what you were thinkin'."

Eugene, miffed, glared at her. "What? You think you're the Queen of England?"

Lizzie sat quietly a moment, her arms straight down to her sides, the fingers of her hands rustling about in half-circle comings and goings. She lowered her head. Tears streamed to her lap.

"Lizzie. I'm…." Eugene placed a hand on her left shoulder, and she pulled away. "I apologize," Eugene said.

"You do not." Lizzie's lower lip extended outwards. The ends of her mouth drooped downward. "You're bein' mean to me."

"Please, I—."

She turned away with abrupt fury. "Mean."

Grumbling, Eugene placed his hands on his hips, looked down onto the bay, and swore. He quickly realized that just the gesture, if not the Queen of England bit, was *indeed* mean. It was a moment of male disregard. Eugene was supposed to be thoughtful in such moments when a lost tourist does

not know where she is and needs assistance. Especially a girl as young…
and as endangered…as Lizzie. With his hands propped up on his hips and
the imperious, disgruntled look out onto the waters, Eugene instead was
treating her with rude indifference, and he knew it. He lowered his hands
and turned back to her.

"I'm sorry," he said. It was a sincere, embarrassed mutter.

"You aren't."

She turned away. Eugene—uniform, badge and all—felt diminished.

"Couldn't you see how scared I was?" Lizzie said.

"Of course."

"I didn't know what they were going to do to me." Lizzie looked up at
Eugene, still frightened. "You know. Even…." She held out her arms and
looked down at her waist. "Well, you know, even—"

"I know."

"But…" She brought a hand to her right cheek. She grimaced while
trying to calm herself. She looked away from Eugene and then looked
back. "They didn't really *do* anything. They just opened up my backpack."
Lizzie brought the still open pack onto her lap. "I thought they wanted my
money, which, you know, wasn't much." She glanced toward Eugene and
even gave him the beginnings of an offer of forgiveness. "After all my
postcards."

"It wasn't for your money?"

"No. It was my passport."

"That's all?"

"They were talkin' about it as they looked it over. The EEU and all that."

"I don't understand."

"They were talking about hearin' me and my granda outside the post
office, and the way we—"

"Your accents?"

"Yeh. And then in the car they were goin' on about selling the passport." She ran a hand through the long hair at the very top of her head. "I
guess you can make money with a passport like that. Even with…even
with…." She leaned forward and placed her elbows on her bent knees. She
took in a watery breath. "Lizzie Daly's dumb passport."

The bay, just now colored a deep, riverine blue, dotted here and there by the white commas of floating gulls, took her attention, while Eugene waited in silence.

"The big guy said…" Lizzie put a finger to her lips. She lowered her voice, an imitation of her abductor. "He said 'Don't you get it? The fuckin' Brexit, see…'" She glanced at Eugene as if to measure how surprised he might be by…disapproving of, maybe…her repeating of the big guy's obscenity. "'We can sell this to some English asshole,' he said to the other eejit." She puzzled a moment, surveying her backpack. "How stupid can you be?" She zipped it shut. "They didn't even look to see if I had a phone." A strained smile appeared on her lips. "Are all Americans as dumb as those two hoors?" She shook her head and looked up at Eugene, actually offering him a difficult smile. "Just catch 'em, that's all…*and* the English hoor, whoever he might be." She sighed, zipped the backpack shut with quiet, angry force, and put it aside. "Some Brit tryin' to get into Heidelberg or somewhere with a picture of me ridin' in his pocket."

Eugene gestured to Lizzie to hand him the backpack. She did, and then stood up herself.

"They're fools, you know, like my granda says." She wiped her eyes.

"The fellows who kidnapped you?"

"Well, them, too. But I mean the English!" Lizzie shook her head with slow relief. Rage remained nonetheless, and Eugene stood quietly, to allow her to be finished with it. "Even though there are a couple English girls in my class at school, and they're all right." She lowered her head. "Diana and Eveline." She wiped her face once more. "Twins."

Eugene continued waiting.

"Not a thing wrong with 'em." She looked down at her clothing, adjusted it, and studied her Doc Martens…. "Is my granda okay?"

"He is. He's waiting for you."

"At the café?"

"Yes. He's worried."

"Yeh." She sobbed once again, a re-angered outburst, and was able quickly to recover from it. She wiped her cheeks and upper lip. "I love him, you know. He's a sweetie." Her voice was still washed by receding tearfulness.

"He didn't have much nice to say about the guys that kidnapped you."

Lizzie lowered her head. Eugene felt from her a semblance of calming, a moment's release from the terror. "Knowin' him, I wouldn't think so," she said.

THE ONLY PLAYBOY

Had he known better what she could do, Raul would have treated Corinth better. And at the moment he still didn't know, despite the fact that he thought he was falling in love with her. He had been watching her this closely just for the previous three hours…their first learning-stage run-through of the play and, he thought, *Love isn't supposed to come on like a lightning strike, is it?*

He sat on a folding chair at the side of the room, watching Corinth rehearse the final moment in *The Playboy of The Western World*. Pegeen Mike, almost in tears, watches Christy Mahon—played by Raul—disappear triumphantly across the far distant bog with his nutcase, thrice-slain father. Just in this brief moment, Raul could see how accomplished an actress Corinth was…how well considered, how deep her understanding of love was, how finely she understood moral failure.

"'*Oh, my grief, I've lost him surely.*'" Pegeen Mike held Christy's scarf, which he had given her, as though it were the stately, sad emblem of the end of love. Her tears now did fall upon it. It was the scarf that Christy wore throughout the play, an emblem of the pluck he had shown killing his father. That admission to Pegeen Mike and the others in the pub led to Raul's favorite line of Christy's in the play, one that he enjoyed acting out physically on stage. "'*I buried him then.*'" The shovel in Raul's hands was imaginary. But because of his talent using it, the audience could easily see it. "'*Wasn't I diggin' spuds in the field?*'"

The scarf was of bright red wool and had formed a kind of playful underscore to Christy's own claims, false though they were, of patricide and revenge against his father.

Raul knew that written lines from a famous play are no substitute for the roil of true love. But Pegeen Mike had said to Christy, "'*And you a fine, handsome young fellow with a noble brow…it's the poets are your*

like—fine, fiery fellows with great rages when their temper's aroused.'"
Just now Raul would like Corinth to say something like that to him off-
stage somewhere, over a glass of wine. He figured that Corinth may not
use the kind of sensational language of which Pegeen Mike is capable. But
if Corinth would just look at him the way she was looking at him in the
run-through when she uttered that line…. She observed him the same way
every time she recited it. Raul, hoping that the gaze was not just the trained
fakery of a gifted actress, rather the real thing, determined to ask her out.

—

"Coffee?"

Raul was also advising the production at the behest of the first-time director Milly O'Mullaly. He was a superb actor, all the reviews of his work
had said. If the movies were ever to find him, he knew his strengths as a
character actor would get him the jobs. Raul did not have the compelling
beauty that leading men often have. But he was so believable as a youthful
bad guy, his black eyes so convincingly expressive, and his body language
so wonderfully, precisely rough, that he sometimes *did* win the girl, simply because she was fascinated by him. He also had a special talent for
English drawing room comedy because he could do accents. In the case of
the *Playboy*, with Milly he was helping the actors with theirs, the County
Mayo version of English being, of course, essential. He knew that if you get
that wrong, you get the whole play wrong. They were rehearsing *Playboy*
for a run at the Curran in San Francisco and, although Corinth had been
friendly enough through their early script discussions and had sought him
out for help with her accent, they had spent little time otherwise together.

"Where?" Corinth said.

"Up Geary Street. There's a place I like up there on Larkin, called Jane."

"Just 'Jane?'"

"Yes."

"Never heard of it." Corinth offered a smile of such sweetness that it
countered the abrupt dismissal that Raul's café suggestion had gotten. He
had decided that this idea of his maybe wasn't—

"I'd love to," she said.

He back-pedaled. "You would?"

"Yes. I've got some questions."

"About what?"

"About whether Christy really loves Pegeen Mike."

"Of course, he does."

"He's not just playing with her? Using her?"

"You think he is?"

"Well, he's clearly not so dumb as he appears at first. Cute. Fascinating. But manipulative." Corinth raised her eyebrows. "A liar!"

"For sure," Raul admitted

"Ay, me *quare* pagan." This she pronounced with the kind of Mayo grittiness and humor that fills the play. "But a clueless liar."

"You see cluelessness in my performance?" Raul muttered.

"Raul…." Corinth pursed her lips and then, after thinking about a response, frowned. "Look, Pegeen Mike herself comes to understand how… duplicitous he is, no? Look at how she berates him there toward the end!" She did not acknowledge Raul's question. Nor did she disagree with it. "Just a suggestion. Can we talk about it a little?"

Raul now wanted even more to have coffee with Corinth. This idea of Christy as a blatantly intentional roué, rather than just a wandering dummy lost in the west of Ireland—and eventually lost in love—could make for even better comedy. Raul loved the idea of playing a handsome buck, clueless maybe, but no less a deceiver. And now Pegeen Mike could be even more fooled by him. Christy finally stands up to his head-sliced father, who nonetheless eventually drags him off across the bog. In the end, they are more drunken compatriots than bullying father and mewling son. But also in the end…with the disappointment that brings this comedy to its close… Christy's lying brio destroys what he and Pegeen Mike have so lovingly declared to each other earlier in the play.

Corinth put on a black sweater. It was very long, so that when she buttoned it down the front, it suddenly seemed like a slim wool dress. The white blouse was buttoned at the neck, its long, pointed collars emphasizing her fine shoulders. The shoulders were framed by the full curls of her brown-red hair, the red of which suggested yet another west of Ireland element in Pegeen Mike's character…all that hape o' water-borne boggers pullin' fish from the frigid sea. Her hair was one of Corinth's great assets, along with her lips, which were being pursued, as it were, by Christy Mahon throughout their comic negotiations.

She took up a shoulder bag and pointed to the way out of the rehearsal room. "So, are we going?"

—

"Why the name?" he asked as they sat down at the counter at Jane. "'Corinth.'"

The café was a favorite of Raul's, who enjoyed the constant youthfulness of its clientele…mostly people in the tech industry, employees of the software companies along the middle stretch of Market Street. So, a lot of youngish men in beards dressed in Levis and other nods to ersatz cowboy-*nuevo* homeless style, especially in the shirt tails hanging out over their belts. Raul sensed that old, dead John Wayne, his favorite of all movie cowboys since he had been a child (even though Wayne himself was long gone by the time Raul was born,) never went around with his shirt untucked. The women in the café were for the most part tattooed, their hair dyed pink and blue, and wore army boots and other graceful fashion. Corinth herself was like something out of *Vogue Paris* by comparison. When they entered Jane, the usually noisy crowd went almost silent for a few moments as she passed between the tables toward the two empty stools at the counter. Corinth herself seemed not to want to acknowledge any of this…her wonderful looks and so on. She was quite calm about them, something else Raul admired in her.

"The name?" she said.

Raul nodded.

"Corinth. I was born there. My parents…they're old hippies."

"Still?

"Still. Even though they live in Brooklyn now."

"Corinth itself lost its charm?"

"I guess so. But, also, there wasn't a lot of work there for a bearded long-hair that spoke no Greek."

"How old were you when you came back?"

"Two."

"Did you like your name?"

"I loved it! Still do!" She pushed back a lock of hair over her right shoulder. "It's so graceful."

This made sense to Raul, who admired how she was playing Pegeen Mike. The Mayo girl is not sophisticated, and sometimes her language reflects no education and a wish to do something else somehow, somewhere away from her father's village pub, preferably in the arms of a murderous fine-lookin' lad like Christy Mahon. But no. She's stuck in the far coastal Mayo cold. The way Corinth was playing her, Pegeen Mike's roughness was softened by her love-struck language and the great urges she feels when it comes to the impetuous Christy. Raul knew that the audience would sympathize with Pegeen Mike because of the way Corinth luxuriated in the girl's passion-driven flights of feeling.

Corinth herself was no country girl. She had had a career as a child actor in New York, in musicals, and actually had spent a year at the Actors Studio. She was now twenty-five, and Hollywood was knocking. It had, however, not yet tried the door itself, and she was maintaining herself with a still very active stage career. What surprised Raul initially was the same thing that surprised others about Raul himself. Corinth, too, could do accents. At Tosca up in North Beach one night, when several of the cast had gathered, they had gone around the table. Someone had suggested a contest in which all the actors would recite one single line in different accents: "*I love the smell of napalm in the morning.*'" There was comic effort and laughter as the utterance made the round. Raul himself dazzled everyone with renditions in rough cockney, Texas panhandle grit, English public-school elegance, Italian New York mobster, *boricua* New York Puerto Rican, and, of course, County Mayo rural Irish. Corinth did almost as well in other accents, including a Bollywood accent from New Delhi. The other competitors around the table all admitted defeat.

Raul walked Corinth home to her apartment on lower Lombard Street.

"How'd you get yours?" she said.

"The accents? Royal Shakespeare. They taught me."

"But you might as well be from Mayo itself, me *auld* flower."

"You too."

"Maybe. But I don't know anything about the place, except…" Corinth looked up the incline to Russian Hill. It was late, and Lombard Street was empty of foot traffic. The fog had come in and settled heavily over this entire part of the city, so that the cars, buildings, and even the streetlamps seemed stifled. "I guess they have fog like this in Ireland."

"I wouldn't know," Raul said.

Corinth fell into silence. For the moment, the only sounds were those of their trudging up the hill.

"Did it ever occur to you that we're phonies?" Corinth said.

The trudging continued.

"How so?"

Corinth poked him with an elbow. "You have a personality of your own, right, Raul?"

"Of course."

She adjusted the scarf around her neck. It was the red one, the same she wore at the end of the play. "No disrespect. But see, I sometimes get lost in all these characters." She glanced toward him. "Have you ever noticed how often, when a celebrated actor is being interviewed somewhere, how little he has to say?" She smiled, although Raul recognized in it a moment of thoughtful comedy. "He can say '*I love the smell of napalm in the morning*' as though it were coming from Olivier himself. But, asked for an original thought of his own, he mumbles. Looks away. Seems stricken with confusion."

"Speak for yourself, Corinth." Raul chuckled.

"Oh, the women have the same problem, often. A line from Tennessee Williams spoken as though it's the end of life itself."

"'*I have always depended on the kindness of*—'"

"Yes. But on her own, otherwise, a lot of mumbling. Or if it's clearly spoken, a lot of nonsense."

"Nonsense doesn't make you a phony, though, does it? Maybe you're just shy," Raul said. "A lot of actors are shy."

Nodding, Corinth put a hand through the crook in Raul's arm. "It's cold, isn't it?" She adjusted the collar of her coat, and they kept walking. "You know, Pegeen Mike is crazy about Christy."

"I do know that."

"Have you ever been crazy about anyone, Raul?"

Raul did not answer at first, although the truth, poised upon the end of his tongue, almost escaped. He caught himself. It was too early. They barely knew each other.

"Have you?"

"I have, yes. But I'm not going to tell you about it."

"Why not?"

Raul sighed.

"You're married, are you?" Corinth said.

"No."

"But in love."

"I think so, yes."

Corinth turned her head and grinned openly at Raul. "You're not sure?"

"I'm sure, yes, but—"

"Are you in love with someone now?"

"Listen, Corinth, I don't think that's—"

"You *are* in love with somebody."

The fog resisted lifting, although a thick breeze came down from the top of Russian Hill. It caused Corinth to shiver once again.

"Are you?" she said.

—

He had been reading the day before…John Donne. *"And who understands? Not me, because if I did, I would forgive it all."* If Raul himself understood, he would be able to forgive every ill-considered trifle that had crossed his mind. He would forgive himself for all such trifles: various slights he had received from others; jealousies he had felt; unwarranted anger here and there. But he worried just now that if he didn't understand love itself,

Corinth would dismiss his ineptitude. And he worried then that he *really* wouldn't be able to forgive himself.

Even though that had been the situation all his life.

He had been born in San Francisco…a boy, an outcome that had disappointed his mother Estelle. She was now a wealthy Burlingame matron who had gone from that early moment to have Raul's two sisters, over whom she had so ruled that neither of *them* understood. They were each married…one to a brain surgeon; the other to a now-suddenly-wealthy start-up technical whiz…and limited their displays of emotion to playing golf and tennis, although never against each other. Raul had not signed up for the U.S. Marine Corps, which had dismayed his father Jalen, who felt that the kinds of ruggedness The Corps had provided for him during "the Vietnam thing" would likewise see Raul through the rigors of business. It had done so for Jalen Kelly, who was a noted venture capitalist…Square, Uber, and so on. Jalen himself had predicted an entrepreneurial business career for his son the moment Raul had struggled from his mother's womb in 1990. "Here. Read this," his father had once ordered him, having finally decided to do something about Raul's preference for novels, poetry, and the footlights. At the time, the boy was sixteen. Before going to sleep, Raul did dip into *The Art of The Deal*, which his father had tossed onto his bed. Trump. Bad writing. Self-obsessed silliness. The boy returned quickly to his Edith Wharton. It had been especially tough for his father when Raul was accepted to the Yale School of Drama, after getting his degree in English from Stanford.

"You want to be an actor!" his father had muttered.

"Yes."

"But both those places have great business schools."

"I know, Dad"

"Like who? Johnny Depp?"

Raul thought it over. "Sure."

"Nah." His father shook his head. "There's no money in that."

—

With every utterance of Pegeen Mike's line, Corinth continued looking at Raul the same way, especially on opening night. The pause he gave before his response to the line, which he improvised himself during that first performance, allowed Christy to respond to Pegeen Mike the way Raul himself wished to respond to Corinth. The pause reflected pleased, accepting surprise.

They had now known each other for two months, and Raul's wishes seemed so unruly to him that he realized he had to tell her what he was feeling. It mattered to him that she might laugh at the outburst and advise him to get his…well, passions together and stick to the task before them. But so be it! he advised himself.

He walked her home after every performance. They talked. There was laughter and shared experience. Patter. Fun. Affection. Until the night Corinth asked Raul if he would like to come up for a glass of wine.

Her phone rang the next morning and Corinth wrestled through her purse for it. Much from the purse got strewn across the bed: a lipstick, some crumpled Kleenex, a small note pad, and a half-filled packet of gum, until the phone finally presented itself. She checked it to see who was calling. "Jesus! It's Hylda."

"Who?"

"My agent."

Corinth lay back against the pillow and brought the phone to her ear. The conversation was a joyous shouting match.

"I got it?" Corinth sat up, leaning forward over the phone. Raul placed a hand on her lower back. She was shaking with excitement. "Which part?"

Hylda spoke at some length. Even Raul could hear the glee in her voice.

"You mean, *the* part?" Corinth grasped the phone with both hands as Hylda continued talking. Raul could tell, from the change of tone in the agent's voice, that more serious issues were coming. "But when do I see the contract?"

More response.

"Tomorrow! You want me to come down there tomorrow?"

The conversation went on for several more minutes. Raul got up, put on his pants, and went into the kitchen to make coffee. When Corinth turned off her phone, he returned to the bedroom. She sat back against a bunched-up pillow. She had put on her blouse and, holding the phone in both hands, was weeping.

"What'd you get?" he said.

She put the phone down on the crumpled sheet to her side. "George Clooney."

"Somebody gave you George Clooney?"

"I'm in his new movie. He's directing."

"Who else is in it?"

"George himself!"

"And you're—"

"He's my father, and he and I are doing the heist together."

"You and George."

"Yes! The Great Mugol Diamond! In Paris!"

Corinth leaned forward and folded her arms. She shook her head, a sparkling of great relief. "Oh, Raul." She reached out for his hand. "Please. A hug." She took him into her arms. "I'm so glad you got to hear this." She kissed his shoulder. "You brought me luck. You're part of it."

The next morning very early, she flew to Los Angeles. She knew she had to get back by mid-afternoon at the latest. Curtain time for *Playboy* was 8:30. Raul drove her to the airport. Corinth was so excited that she could talk about little else.

"What if this…? What if….?" She put on her sunglasses and, with them, Raul saw the star quality that now, suddenly, possessed her. He wondered if there had been an actual change in her, or if he were simply viewing her with the aid of her…her… He considered the words. *Her moment!* Yes, she was an actress. Yes, she had beauty that, as Milly O'Mullaly had said when they first met, "could kill." But since her telephone conversation with Hylda the morning before, Corinth's very bearing had changed, and staring out the windshield as they descended Hyde Street toward the freeway, Raul was indeed discomfited. He grumbled in silence. He felt his stomach tighten. He knew what it was. Jealousy nudged him and identified itself.

Corinth Jamison! right up there on the movie poster, above the title with George. Two hoods working a caper, both beyond gorgeous, Corinth on the way to her first Oscar.

Plain jealousy.

That afternoon Raul was late picking her up at the airport. He did ask her what the meeting with Hylda…and, as it happened, George…was like. Corinth flooded the conversation with details.

"He is such a nice man!" "Well, they're excited too. Imagine! *They're* excited!" "No, he wasn't in the limousine at the airport. But they did send a limousine. Imagine. For me!" "They hadn't seen as good a screen test as mine in, well, ever!"

Raul chatted, but that was it. His own career floated past him as Corinth spoke. Now it seemed amateur to him. Way back in the back as an actor, and not a gifted one. Maybe his father was right. Raul, wasting his time in regional theaters, going nowhere. Sitting alone with a bowl of buttered popcorn on his lap, he would watch Corinth, on television, hurry up to the stage at the Academy Awards, to thank her parents the long-hair and the hippie mom, to thank George, to thank Hylda, and not a word about Raul Kelly. By then, I'll be her ex-boyfriend, among others. Nothing much.

"You know, I wish you had been there," Corinth said.

Distracted, Raul glanced toward her, and saw she was worried about what he was thinking.

"I mean, I'm telling you all this, and maybe it's too much."

"It's your day, Corinth. Don't worry about me."

"But I think I'm—"

"My day's coming."

"I'm sure it is, but I just think—"

Raul's fingers tightened around the steering wheel. "Don't worry about it!" He kept his eyes on the freeway ahead.

Corinth turned her eyes ahead also. Sadness pervaded her silence. They spoke little for the rest of the trip into town.

—

The next morning, Milly O'Mullaly wanted to talk with both of them to-gether at the theater.

"Look, we all know what's going on."

"You do!" Corinth said. The outburst faltered as it left her lips, as though tears were about to follow.

"Everyone does, Corinth. And after last night's lousy performance? Are you two kidding? And the worst of it in situations like this is that it affects what everyone else is doing. So…"

Milly had grown up in County Galway and Dublin and, after emigrating to the States, had gained a reputation for stand-up comedy in New York City. She was known for the hilarious fun she made of LGBTQ people, justified by the fact that she herself *was* one. She had voiced her dependence on Raul and Corinth both as they had ventured through the early *Playboy* rehearsals. They had such experience as actors that Milly freely admitted how much she needed their help on this, her directorial debut. As the rehearsals had progressed, however, she had come into her own, and now she was indeed *the* director. She also seemed to know County Mayo like the back of her hand. Both actors had acquiesced, realizing how good Milly really was.

Perturbed, she allowed her eyes to close for a moment. She was angry with both and was thinking how best to proceed. Heavy-set, in fine athletic condition, she usually dressed in an extra-large T-shirt with a fiery left-wing progressive demand of some sort printed on the front, purple gym tights and black leather loafers, white socks. When working, she piled her long black hair up in a curl-ridden pyramid at the top of her head. Her formidable smile enhanced the gifts she had for immediate hilarity on-stage.

But she was not in the mood for any of that just now.

She removed her horn-rimmed glasses and lay them on the table before her. "So, I want the two of you to grow up."

Now Corinth did begin weeping.

"Corinth!"

The downward-turning tone of voice caused even more tears. Raul reached across the table for the box of Kleenex resting on it and slid it toward Corinth. She glanced at him with a look of squashed gratitude and took several of them.

"And you, Raul." Milly sat back and folded her arms before her. It was clear to Raul that the director thought him responsible for the lovers' quarrel and Corinth's unhappiness. He would beg to differ, but also knew that men *usually* beg to differ in these kinds of situations, even though they so frequently *are* responsible. Raul knew that any protest he could make would bring instant opprobrium down upon him, especially from Milly. He considered reaching for the Kleenex himself.

"We have a closin' night tonight. The place is sold out. It's been sold out the whole time, for Lord's sake. You are superb together. Corinth just got that offer." Milly leaned over the table and entwined her hands together. "You're lovers."

"You know about that?" Corinth whimpered.

"What do you think, we're all blind?" Her fingers resembled hunkered down disapproval. "What else do the two of you want?"

Raul grumbled. He raised a hand to interrupt.

"Put an end to this bickerin', Raul. Be nice!" Milly then fixed her gaze on Corinth and Raul both, each equally. "Move on." There would be no denials. "Give up the moody broodin', will youse? and do your job."

—

The curtain opened on a dark stage. The lighting slowly revealed the interior of the shabby Irish village pub. A few wooden tables and chairs. No paint on the wall boards. No décor. A few small windows. The bar…more a country-store counter, the lower reaches of which were stained by years of spilled Guinness and the scrapes of rough boots…had a large bottle and two rough ceramic mugs on it and an old, piled-up rag. The pub was beset by poverty.

Offstage, Corinth wiped her eyes with the hem of her apron. In thirty seconds, she had to go on. She glanced to the right, where Milly and Raul stood watching in back-stage semi-darkness. She dropped the apron and took up the list on which she would be writing as she entered the pub. For a second or two she seemed ready to break down. But she pursed her lips, gathering herself, and reached for the doorknob that would open her way to the pub and to the first act of *The Playboy of The Western World*.

Her performance was the best of the play's run, especially as, at the end, she approached the front of the stage and gathered her hands before her. Pegeen Mike's voice had become a glistening surge. Her shoulders lowered and she seemed barely able to speak. She took up the end of her red scarf and wiped her cheeks with it. Letting it drop, she looked toward the window that was open to a view of the bog in the distance.

"*'Oh, my grief, I've lost him surely.'*"

The theater was silent. The audience seemed not to be breathing. Pegeen Mike put a hand into the pocket of her apron and took out the list from which she had been reading at the beginning of the first act. She looked it over, crumpled it, and put it back in the pocket. Standing alone in the pub's rural light, she turned to face the audience, and looked out into the far away. She wrung her hands.

"*'I've just lost the only playboy of the western world.'*"

She sorrowed as the lights went abruptly black, and Raul, by now off-stage again and still feeling the betrayal he had so vividly enacted upon Pegeen Mike, realized his own very stupid error.

The audience remained silent for a moment, as though not grasping what they had seen. Finally, their applause burst onto the now re-lit, empty stage.

As the cast came out for a bow, Corinth, still in the midst of her sadness, reached for Raul's hand. He kept hers in his throughout the curtain calls and, finally, in the middle of the fifth one, in which just he and Corinth came out on stage to noise and acclaim, he brought it to his lips. Corinth allowed the moment. He looked into her eyes. "Forgive me. Please," he whispered.

Blowing kisses at the audience, thrilled with their applause, washed over with cheers, Corinth yet turned to Raul. "Come with me."

He realized that he had not seen even Pegeen Mike, in the midst of her happiest, enthralled moments with Christy Mahon, appear so overtaken by love.

SECRETOS

"Arlo, life's too short, man." Cruz laid his glasses on the desk and rested the side of his head on his right palm, looking out the window. "Too short."

He took in a breath as Arlo nattered a reply. This was the second gig in a month that Cruz had gotten for *Arlo y Los Locos* to which the band had arrived late. This time, Arlo explained, the Express Passenger had broken down. The Express Passenger was an aging Chevrolet van, quite used, from Arlo's cousin Lester Bedoya in Daly City, which the band's rising promise had allowed them to buy. They had removed all the seats in order to carry the band's equipment, Arlo at the wheel. The other musicians, for whom there was no room in the van, would arrive in whatever way they could. The previous excuse, a month before, had been that the Siena had broken down. The Siena was an even older Toyota vehicle that the band had named *El Barco de Los Locos*, borrowed from Lester. It too had no seats.

At least on this second occasion, just the night before, the band *had* arrived, although an hour late. The first time, the band had not shown up at all, and Arlo had actually traded blows with the club owner the next day, on an Oakland street corner, who had insulted him for being Puerto Rican. This time, the owner of the restaurant/bar on Mission Street in San Francisco, a friend of Cruz's father from Argentina, had shorted the band on its money because of their tardiness—"I had to do bird whistles, Arlo!" —and the other guys in the band had had to escort Arlo out of the place after the gig, so that he wouldn't threaten the Argentine as well.

The musicians in the band were terrific, Arlo himself a timbales player of real note even though he was only twenty-two. But he had taken over the management of the band as well, from Joe Corteza, the pianist who had his head on straight, had two kids, no drug issues, and could organize the band well enough to get them to gigs on time. Arlo had recently fired Joe, jealous of the band's dependence upon the older man's more steady demeanor, and the fortunes of *Arlo y Los Locos* had begun to wane.

During Arlo's explanation, Cruz surveyed Minnesota Street out the window, and the buildings across the way. His small talent-booking office was on the second floor of an old factory building now filled with art galleries. The Dogpatch neighborhood was becoming avant-garde, judging from the art, and one with posh visitors, judging from the prices for the art... self-important on both scores. Comely young, aggressive, artfully dressed women walked around everywhere in his building...gallery employees, a daily excitement for the twenty-six-year-old Cruz. The fashionable bohemian look of the many gallery visitors belied the clear poverty of the occasional artist seen sneaking around.

Arlo's anger caused Cruz's mind to wander, and he had a sudden, affectionate recollection.

Twenty years ago, he had often visited this same building, which had had a different purpose then. His father Erwin Goyeneche had been the daytime shop foreman of a post office processing plant on the ground floor. Cruz had loved the sound of the loose planking when he would walk across the shop floor on weekends, hand in hand with his father, when the machinery was silent. His father would have extra paperwork to do, and would bring Cruz along for company. It was a sound that child and father both enjoyed, especially when Cruz had been challenged by his father to find the squeakiest floor plank of them all. There had been thousands of thick planks, all of them many years old, most of them worn down along the edges, thick, warped, and poorly painted.

"*Che chico,* look around. You'll find it." His father would come out of the office now and then, to supervise the search. With so many loose planks, the quest was complicated and, for the boy, serious fun. Cruz could never be sure which was the loosest. The day Cruz finally found The Number One Plank, as Erwin had called it, Erwin brought him back to the office, sat him down across the desk, and brought an envelope from a desk drawer. Cruz tore it open and found a paper sticker with an illustration of The Virgin Mary on it, like the ones they gave out to the best students every Friday at Our Lady of The Visitation school, where Cruz was in the first grade. She smiled, The Virgin did, looking down dreamily from a swirling cloud. There were also two dollars in the envelope.

"You deserve it, *chico,*" Erwin said.

Cruz ran around the desk and hugged his father. He pocketed the two dollars and told Erwin that he would stick the sticker onto his bedroom mirror. Cruz still had the mirror, in his own apartment in San Francisco. While The Virgin Mary had faded badly, and parts of the paper had fallen away at the edges, she still held a kind of deteriorated court over Cruz's bedroom.

During the week, millions of pieces of paper, envelopes, letters, personal packages, messages from home, messages to home, greeting cards, birthdays cards and every other sort of mailed item swirled, were processed, and flew through all the post office machinery, Monday through Friday, eventually brought together in neat, paper-banded groupings that were then dumped into large canvas mailing bags. The noise in the shop made speech almost impossible. There was such a clattering metronomic racket everywhere that, of course, Cruz could not actually hear the squeak of The Number One Plank when he would visit during the week. But this was another order of thrilling excitement for the boy. Even in such chaos, his hand held tightly by his father so that he would not wander toward the dangerous machines, he could feel the press of the loose plank against the bottom of his shoe and, so, knew that it was squeaking. The sound itself was a secret...knowable, the little boy thought, only to his father and himself. Cruz had often thought since then that no memory could be so pedestrian, yet so deeply evocative of the feelings he had for his father.

The caress by the wood of the bottom of his Converse tennis shoe.

His father Erwin, whom he loved for the way he danced and, especially, the way he dressed when he danced—the perfectly ironed white dress-shirt, the jet-black silk necktie and just as black double-breasted suit, the black suede dance shoes with suede soles, his straight black hair laid flat against his skull with shiny Pomade—was Cruz's connection to his aunts, uncles and cousins back in Buenos Aires. Erwin was the man who had begun Cruz's journey toward becoming a stellar *asador.* His father was noted especially for his rosemaried lamb, and was to give Cruz more than a dozen not-to-be-shared recipes for *chimichurri.* Those Sunday afternoon *asados* had also featured tango, of which Erwin was an *aficionado*. Born in the Villa Urquiza neighborhood of Buenos Aires, Erwin had wished to be in the military, and joined the Argentine army in 1980. Two years later, he was wounded in the Malvinas War, during the defense of the Stanley airfield, a bad flesh wound to the right of his stomach. He had lain on a stretcher for two days, the medics having run out of supplies. The head-wounded medic lying on a stretcher next to him died just before the evacuation finally began, and Erwin always remembered looking back at the fellow as they carried Erwin to a helicopter. The dead medic was dressed in his ripped, mud-stained fatigues, lying perfectly still on the stretcher, his skull wrapped in bandages stained brown with dried blood, crusted here and there with dead flies. Erwin was flown back to the mainland and, a few months after the Argentine defeat, was mustered out of the army, with a medal for valor.

Cruz himself was born in San Francisco in 1985, the same year his parents arrived in the U.S.

With time, Erwin instructed Cruz in tango. Erwin expertly essayed multiple *agujas*, *amagues* and *boleos* with rough, legible grace, and had been noted especially by the professional *tangueros* in Buenos Aires for his rough *milonguero* abilities, added now and then to his more elegant *Villa Urquiza* softness. Erwin danced with considerable grace, with a humorous helping of street-cool danger tossed in. When the boy was eight years old and attending his first summer *milongas* in the patio behind their house in Visitation Valley, being led through the dance by his father, he understood right away what Erwin defined as "*la inténsidad*, Cruz. *La atención.*"

Erwin died in Buenos Aires while visiting a dying cousin when Cruz was 10. Recalling this now, the telephone still held to his ear, Cruz felt his eyes turning to glisten, and he laid his forehead onto the fingers of his right hand. Arlo, still making a defense of himself, didn't notice, and kept talking.

—

Cruz danced tango occasionally with Julietta Medina, a woman who had had three husbands, two of whom she had left. The third was Benjamin Arden, a retired American investment banker, a tall and quiet New Englander who had attended Choate and Yale. He was quite well spoken despite his shyness, gray-haired and usually clothed in New England tweed, a blue dress shirt and an old-school tie. He treated Julietta with extraordinary kindliness. He was many years older than she. They lived on Jackson Street in Pacific Heights and were of such polished elegance that they seemed simply out of place dancing the Argentine tango, so beautiful a dance, so working class....

When he danced tango, Cruz made a point of dressing more conservatively than he did when he was booking music acts. He shopped at Macy's downtown, always buying from his mother's cousin Marco. Marco would call Cruz when a special sale was going on and would put things aside for him. So...when he danced tango, Cruz wore black suits from Kenneth Cole, the closest things to Hermes ties and handkerchiefs that Marco could gather together, Cole-Haan Collections shoes (always black, and always resoled with suede), glasses with special Yves Saint Laurent black frames, and a Rolex watch that had been the only luxury item his father had ever owned...a gift from Erwin's Buenos Aires cousin Polaco. With his tall, smoothly slim body and somewhat Iranian-style good looks, and especially because of his gentlemanly kindness on the dance floor, Cruz never lacked for dance and conversation at the *milongas*.

Julietta was of Paraguayan extraction, very dark with extremely dark eyes, who was known among the tango people in San Francisco as a silent queen-like beauty who kept to herself. She dressed only in fashionable, museum-board designer luxury, noted by the other women dancers for her shoes, which she bought exclusively—and very often—from an Argentine company of considerable fame itself named Comme il faut. She spoke no Spanish, having been raised in East Side Manhattan on Fifth Avenue, across from Central Park. Julietta and Benjamin had a great deal of money, and had traveled the world, staying in the most remarkable hotels anyone could imagine. They had once described for Cruz how they received an expensive gift every Christmas from the general manager of the Danieli in Venice, where they stayed for a month each year. A hand-written letter as well from that same general manager.

Julietta was so fine a tango dancer that she was complimented for the sensuous flow just of her walk. Her walk was itself a composed dance.

One evening, Cruz and she were dancing at The Verdi Club, to the tango *Tengo miedo*, recorded by Ada Falcón with the orchestra of Francisco Canaro. This tango is no longer well known, but Falcón sings it in such a way that Cruz felt it to be an undiscovered treasure. The lyrics tell of a woman afraid to love her lover. The irony of the performance is that, when Falcón declares her fear, she does so with a smile in her voice.

Cruz asked Julietta if she knew the lyrics to this tango. When she replied that she did not, he translated them for her as they danced.

Tengo miedo... "I'm afraid..." A pause, in which he could feel Falcon's search for the correct words, which she delivered with considerable enjoyment, as though she were looking up at her lover and saying, with a smile, "Yes. Yes, I will." *"Tengo miedo...de quererte."* *"I'm afraid...to love you."*

Toward the end of the tango, Cruz sensed that the emotional state in which he and Julietta had begun dancing had changed. For one thing, the front of his suit jacket was damp. The music came to an end, and as he released Julietta from the embrace he saw that she was in tears.

"It's just that...your translation...it reminded me of my father," she explained. "I...I so loved him."

"What did he do?" Cruz asked.

"Oh..." Julietta shrugged. "He was unusual for someone from Paraguay. He was in shipping. He owned ships." She put the fingers of her right hand to her lips as she surveyed the dance floor. She wore a ring of black jade. "I stopped seeing him after I finished school. Sarah Lawrence. He wanted to see me. But I refused. I was very mean to him. And then...then he died."

"What happened?" Cruz asked.

"I think...I think he died of sadness." She sighed, looking for a moment at the ring, caressing it with her fingers. "Because he'd lost me."

The following day, Julietta and Benjamin took Cruz to the Britex Fabrics store on Post Street downtown. The staff knew the location of each remnant in the store—a store filled with thousands of such remnants—where each bolt of cloth was, each button, each sequin. The store was long, very narrow, and so well-tended that Julietta had seldom succeeded in finding a speck of dust in any remnant that she bought.

Julietta shopped there for embroidery and brocade, cloth that reminded her, she said, of her mother, who had died long ago in Paraguay, when Julietta had been twelve. She and Benjamin invited Cruz to tea afterwards in their home, and Julietta told him about the messages she had received from her mother, when she had been a little girl.

Her mother and father had been divorced, and her father had basically stolen the girl and brought her to New York. He had forbidden his former wife to visit them or to talk to Julietta on the phone. So, the mother had sent letters to Julietta that she had sewed into remnants of embroidered lace and brocaded silk. The letters were secret. All her father knew was that his ex-wife was sending Julietta the sewn gifts, and he allowed the girl to receive them. Julietta suspected that his doing so absolved him of the guilt he must have felt being so cruel to his daughter and his wife. Each letter was a soulfully made present to a little girl far away, and each one of them made her suffer terribly.

—

Erwin's cousin Polaco's real name was Roberto Goyeneche. Erwin had at least been able to visit this cherished, famous relative—one of the greatest ever singers of Argentine tango—before Roberto died in 1994. Roberto was followed quickly by Erwin himself, who had a heart attack the day after the singer's funeral. The last memory that Cruz had of his father was that of laying his forehead against the side of Erwin's closed coffin, returned to San Francisco from Buenos Aires. Cruz's mother Geraldín's right hand patted the back of his head, caressing the boy.

Erwin Goyeneche had often reminisced about his cousin Roberto. He was known as "Polaco" because of his pale skin and his skinniness. Erwin's favorite of Polaco's recordings was that of the tango *Muchacho*, about a little boy who does not yet know the sadness of losing love, or what would come to him when he finally found love.

"Children," Cruz's father would say listening to the tune, his eyes seeming far away in reminiscence. "They know so little, *hijo*...especially about love."

When he learned that Erwin had died, Cruz knew that his father had been wrong about that. Cruz's soul melted within him when his mother told him that "your daddy's..." Geraldín, sitting next to Cruz on his bed, was unable to cry any longer. "He's gone."

A few days after the news, Geraldín sat with Cruz on the couch in their living room. She leaned far forward and pressed the palms of her hands against her eyes. She had an opened letter in her right hand. She lay it on her lap and read from it, a description by her sister-in-law of how Erwin had died. "We had been dancing a tango, in Uncle Cacho's house, for the memory of Polaco. Erwin was always so good at tango. And fifteen minutes later he was gone. So alive in one moment…and the next, his soul suddenly vanished. *¡Ay Geraldín! Erwinito murió y nadie….*" His aunt had been unable to complete the sentence. Cruz laid his hands on his mother's, which had crumpled a corner of the letter, himself wishing to run from this duty, that there be no need for it, that his father be alive and take his wife into his arms, to dance.

A priest eulogized Erwin in the Our Lady of The Visitation parish church. Cruz himself spoke at the funeral, but could not finish. Now, years later, still looking out his office window, still muttering imprecations at *Arlo y Los Locos*, Cruz recalled a visit to their house by Polaco himself, on tour from Argentina, and a musician friend of whom Cruz's father had been a true fan, a man who had written an immortal piece about his own father's death entitled *Adios Nonino*. Cruz, five years old, had been stunned by his father's surprised, noisy amazement when the other musician had come in the front door of the house behind the celebratory, much-welcomed Polaco.

"*Maestro* Astor," Erwin whispered, shaking his head and taking Astor into his arms. "Welcome!" He turned toward Cruz. "*¡Chico! ¡Imagináte!* Astor Piazzolla!"

Erwin had to explain to the boy who Astor was, and when Polaco and Astor stayed for lunch—spaghetti *al limón y crema*, a salad of tomatoes, mozzarella cheese and sweet basil, salted, peppered and sprinkled with olive oil, and a great large loaf of Italian bread that they all broke up with their hands—Astor asked that the child sit next to him. He accepted a hunk of bread with a large clod of butter on it that Cruz had constructed for him. Polaco and Astor both complimented Geraldín's rustic cooking, especially the quality of freshness of her home-grown tomatoes, which, in Astor's words, "leant music to this salad, *señora.*" Later in the afternoon, Erwin described that particular Saturday as the most important day in his life. "Except, of course, the day you were born, *mi'jo*," his father hurried to say to the un-offended, equally happy Cruz.

—

Julietta showed Cruz several of her mother's letters. She had catalogued them by date and had stored them singly in protective manila envelopes. The letters themselves contained bits of family news and were written in very simple Spanish. Each was framed in cloth, pink, green, light blue, made playful by the lace that her mother had sewn to the cloth, by the colored thread that held the lace to the paper, by little tassels, cloth buttons, quilted little squares of velvet, gold brocade, bright cotton and silk, silver and white.

"The maid had to read them to me," Julietta told Cruz. "In secret, of course. I couldn't understand the Spanish."

"Why haven't you ever learned Spanish?"

"I couldn't stand it! Spanish was my father's language, even though he spoke English to me. He spoke Spanish on the phone every day, doing business. It was like a gun or something. He was always so formally dressed, shirt and tie. Perfect. His black hair combed, so handsome. And everything he said on the phone sounded so threatening." Julietta's lips pursed, turned down. "Condemning." She let out a breath. "I refuse to speak…the Spanish." She smiled, her lips quivering with grief. "That's what he called it. 'The Spanish'".

Cruz read a few of the letters, translating out loud into English the forty-year-old news about the new bishop at the cathedral, about her mother's servant Locala, a Guaraní Indian woman who made such wonderful coffee, and Locala's sister Marisol who had six little children, all of whom prayed every Sunday for Julietta's soul.

Julietta nodded, joyful in the memories. When Cruz looked up at her, she was seated in the sunlight coming in a window, on a chair for which she had done the needlepoint work on the chair-back herself, a pair of dark red roses on an ebony background. Benjamin sat across from her, a saucer and cup of tea in his hands. He had heard this story many times before, it was obvious. But he listened in silence nonetheless, allowing Julietta her sorrow.

She had handed the woman at Britex a fifty-dollar bill, to pay for a selection of colorful remnants, a few pearlescent buttons, some red velvet tassels and a quite frayed but nonetheless somberly beautiful piece of blue Chinese silk. The clerk put the items into a white plastic sack and handed it to her with the change, thanking her without looking at her.

The three shoppers passed back into the flow of Post Street.

"What do you do with the remnants?" Cruz asked as they stood before the shop awaiting Benjamin's driver. The folded cloth showed through the plastic, as though shrouded by a cold fog.

For a moment, Julietta remained silent. "I donate them to the Catholic girls' school in my neighborhood." She put on her sunglasses. "You know, Sacred Heart Convent, on Broadway. For the girls' art classes." She looked back over her shoulder at the store windows. "I like their selection here. Their prices. They've got everything." The glasses hid her eyes. "But mostly, Cruz," she murmured, "I come here to weep."

—

Once he was able to get Arlo off the phone, Cruz sat silently as he recalled his father sitting in his office in the processing plant, a week or so following the boy's discovery of The Number One Plank. Erwin wore a white shirt and tie and was looking out the window onto the shop floor. Cruz and Geraldín were visiting. Cruz, as always, was amazed by the rush of so many pieces of paper through so much cockeyed machinery.

"Each of those envelopes contains something, no, Cruz?" Erwin said. "They're like tangos, no? Like Astor's tangos. Each one with some surprise. With a secret, a heart of some kind." He laughed. "*Secretos*." His thin, dark face broadened with a smile. "Secrets. *¿No te rompen la cabeza?* That's like saying in English…like…something like 'Don't they drive your heart crazy?'"

Because of the mystery of it, the boy had always cherished the question, and still did.

MARY INOCENCIA

"I'm leavin'." Paco took up his skateboard and moved toward the front door.

"Good!" His former friend DJ Yo had just called him a dumb Mex.

"And I'm Salvadorean," Paco muttered.

"So what? What's the difference?"

Paco had incurred Yo's wrath because he had not wished to loan the… *Well, he* is *a gringo, isn't he?*…the *gringo* his skateboard. So, their friendship had been ruined in just this last moment. Yo had quit high school a few years ago, while Paco was in his second year at the San Francisco Art Institute… on full scholarship. He had painted his own skateboard, which was the reason he did not lend it out. He had even been talking to Kryptonics about a couple of designs for them…a version of the Virgin of Guadalupe contemplating heaven's clouds and another of the long-ago assassinated Archbishop Òscar Romero offering his blessing, buffeted by clouds of gore. Kryptonics had turned him down, although apparently realizing that more and more *Latinx* kids have money these days. They had asked Paco to send more ideas.

Paco and Yo had been skateboarding together for the last year, primarily in the Ferry Building plaza at the foot of Market Street. There was reason for this. The plaza is very large and smooth, which makes it a natural for practicing. Also, pedestrians cross back and forth across the plaza all day long…lots of them. So, the game they had of intertwining their courses through and past all these people was a lot of fun for the two nineteen-year-olds. Both were expert boarders, and both could get away quick in case they blazed past someone a little too closely or got threatened by some dark-suit lawyer and his friends returning to their offices from lunch.

"Fuck their offices," as Yo liked to put it.

—

Sister Mary Inocencia so loved the ocean that she visited it at least once a month. The Pacific, that is. She hastened to make the distinction between this and any other ocean, even though the only other one she had visited was the Atlantic. Between them she felt there was no comparison. She had grown up in Glendale, California, and the Pacific had welcomed her into its arms almost from the day of her birth. Her father had taken her swimming for the first time in Santa Monica when she was two, and often described for his daughter her laughter on that occasion, the ocean seeming to provide her with pure, splashing fun. Although that specific thrill was beyond her memory, she well remembered the hundreds of following visits during her childhood and adolescence.

But in 1962, as a thirteen year-old, Mary Laverty began to be embarrassed by wearing a bathing suit. She gave up that item of wear when she made her first profession of vows in 1969, but she always recalled being so…thirteen! and luxuriating in the warmth of the Santa Monica sun against the backs of her legs. She would lay on a large towel, accompanied by her mother and sister Eve on their own towels, her mother's mild skin protected from the sun by the shade of a large beach umbrella. The sunlight would strew itself across Mary like the very essence of pleasure itself. Not entirely protected from the eyes of boys by her mother, she was embarrassed by the bathing suit and how much of herself it revealed. She found the sun nonetheless to be the closest of friends…an intimate, if the truth be told. It reminded her of the other solitary enjoyments that she kept to herself. Actually, the sun was an adviser to her on the entire subject of earthly pleasures.

Mary had been told by The Church that such notions would send you to hell and, despite the sweets they offered, she felt she had to turn her back on them. The Church told her to. But also, she worried how such things came from "the Devil's dirty mind," as Sister Mary Gabriel, the principal at Holy Family High had assured the girls, and surely Sister Mary Gabriel knew more about these things than did Mary Laverty.

An honors student at Holy Family, Mary discovered her vocation as a nun at about the same time she abandoned her last bathing suit. But she could not abandon the Pacific. Except for The Holy Trinity Themselves, the ocean was her major source of internal happiness. Even now, at the age of seventy and living with other retired nuns on Lone Mountain, she would drive out to the beach at the foot of Golden Gate Park and revel in the view of all those waves off San Francisco, so many of them, by the thousands over and over forever. She had taught school for some years in El Salvador, a missionary with the Maryknoll Sisters, and the experience had introduced her to even deeper prayers for deliverance, mostly as a result of the civil war there. She had loved El Salvador, even becoming reasonably fluent in Spanish. The people…the Central American combination of celebration and grave sadness, all in the same moment…. She had never met people like them anywhere. But the dreamy promise of an ascension to heaven that the Pacific Ocean offered her was not to be realized in La Libertad, even though the view she had had from the window of her bedroom in the nuns' communal home there had featured restful seaside peacefulness. It was pure Pacific pleasure.

But in December 1980, she had suffered the worst thing she had ever seen, and it had happened just outside La Libertad.

She had recovered only after two following years of emotional abandonment and search in Southern California. During that time, she had come to depend on being picked up a weekend a month from the convent in Monrovia by her cousin Harry, who with his wife and children had a summer place in Newport Beach. There she could walk with her friend Sister Eveline to the Balboa pier, from which the two nuns could marvel with each other, stunned by how this beautiful ocean never seemed to change. "So blue," Mary would say, as she had said lying on the Santa Monica beach as a girl. So refreshing. So filled with love. After La Libertad, though, even this had not been an easy task. She missed the sea. She missed the sun. She even missed her bathing suit. But she suffered from what had happened in El Salvador, in ways the Pacific Ocean would never be able to understand.

—

Paco boarded up the sidewalk that runs along the seawall at the foot of Golden Gate Park. He had been doing so regularly, although Spanishtown, the commune in which he lived out Third Street in Dogpatch, was much farther from the beach than his grandmother Edwina's house on Forty-second Avenue had been. But he liked it in Spanishtown: a warren of rooms, stairways, hallways, and jerry-built kitchens, built from wood and found doors, used appliances, lamps, beds, used mattresses and other detritus, on three floors of an abandoned warehouse. About fifty young artists lived there.... Well, many of them declared themselves artists, but Paco knew that few of them actually were. Just saying you were an artist did not make you one. Four chords poorly essayed on a used guitar (Yo's specific talent) didn't make him into Eric Clapton. Of course, Yo himself didn't even know who Eric Clapton was, the great Englishman now being a grizzled old man beyond the education of most of the residents of Spanishtown. If they knew about him at all, it was as an historical oddity. *Eric Clapton, yeah, wasn't he...was he a Beatle? Didn't he....?* But Paco knew about Clapton, astonished by all those ancient vinyls Edwina's boyfriend, John, had given him and asked him to cherish. Their scuffed, faded covers showed the ancient guitarist as a hippy kid. *I'll bet it was fun being a hippy*, Paco thought. He worried about his grandmother, though, and thought John, who was loving, considerate, and seventy-three, just right for her.

Paco's grandfather Santiago Godoy, Edwina's only husband, had been a banker in San Salvador, and had been killed in the civil war, picked off by an FMLN sniper. He was trying to escape from a bank robbery attempt by the same FMLN. The terrorists did not much distinguish between this person or that stepping from a bank, since banks were the known dens of capitalist *cerotes sinvergüenzas.* Anyone emerging from one was a fair target, especially if he were wearing a suit. Edwina still kept a small altar in her bedroom, on her dresser, which contained two weathered framed studio photos. One, a black and white, yellowed and water-stained along the bottom edge, showed Santiago in coat and tie. He was about thirty-five, formal, and, judging from the picture, happy. The photo rested on a round cotton lace doily. A rosary lay in circular rest before the picture, its small wooden crucifix in repose on top.

Edwina had escaped from El Salvador after her husband's murder, threatened herself by the FMLN. She had had to leave her little baby Simón behind with her mother, and had entered the U.S. illegally in 1982.

The second photo was much newer, in color, and had been taken at a wedding in San Salvador. It showed the bride and groom, Simón and Rosa Godoy, youthful and overjoyed. Simón too wore a suit and tie. Rosa's white wedding dress seemed to glow everywhere, and added emphasis to her dark, quite girlish beauty, especially in her eyes that, Paco knew, he had inherited. Edwina cried about her daughter-in-law's eyes, grasping Paco's hands whenever they looked at the altar together. The photos were bordered by two unlit white candles in Mexican tin holders.

The altar had been on Edwina's dresser for as long as Paco could remember. He worried about his grandmother because she worried so much about him. Paco had been a good boy, always polite and always playing with crayons and watercolors when he was little. Edwina liked all that. But she was chronically over-concerned about everything. Paco knew that, even if he had graduated at the top of his high school class at Lick Wilmerding (indeed he had come in fourth, behind the Lopez twins, Marianita and Luz Rosario, and Harvey Chan) his grandmother would have thought his coming in first wasn't enough. She hadn't helped him enough with his homework. The clothes he wore weren't pressed well enough. She couldn't afford that computer he had asked her for. If only she could have brought her son Simón with her when she had snuck into the United States…. Edwina anguished, always. Maybe God was punishing her for her abandonment so long ago of her own little boy.

Paco's coal-black hair was riven with long curls. "Just like your mother's," Edwina often assured him, fingering the curls. Simón and Rosa had died in the northern Sonoran desert, trying to make it to the U.S. border in 2002. The Mara Salvatrucha gang in San Salvador had shaken Simón down, and threated Rosa's life if he didn't pay. When little Paco himself, just two years old, finally did get across, cared for by a couple of other immigrants, a sympathetic U.S. border patrol guy, and some Catholic Church volunteers, Edwina came from San Francisco to get him. Flooded with grief for her lost son and daughter-in-law, her first sight of Paquito had caused even more grief, which had never left her, ever.

Paco was the only *latinx* in Spanishtown, and he might as well not have been *latinx*, for all that the others cared. They were young *gringos* who, like most *gringos*, didn't know or seldom asked what kind of *latinx* Paco actually was. Not real smart, most of them, although they *were* artists! Now and then, one of them asked him what the Spanish word was for something. Otherwise they expected him to like the same music they liked, the same drugs, the same tattoos, and the same raggedy clothes. Yes, he was *latinx*, but they were white and did not seem interested in what made Paco not white.

El Salvador? Where's that?

—

He surged and swerved up the sidewalk, the Cliff House the beacon toward which he was aiming. Paco enjoyed the sounds the board made as he wove his way, rising and lowering in intensity as the wheels dug through a turn or floated in a straight line. The sounds resounded for him the way those from the waves did, so constant as their roar floated in from the great beach's shore break.

Paco hurried and relaxed, propelled himself and slowed, looking to his left now and then to enjoy the ocean. He didn't notice the old woman stepping up onto the sidewalk from the crosswalk that crossed the Great Highway. She barely saw him coming. She yelled and held out her arms to ward him off. But Paco collided with her, knocking her to the cement.

The skateboard skittered off and banged into the seawall. Paco himself planted a leg, careened to the side, and fell. He scraped the palms of both hands and banged his right elbow. Everything hurt as he rolled up the sidewalk. He panicked, thinking that the woman must be injured too, and hurried to his hands and knees.

"Jesus, I'm sorry!"

Mary's eyes were open. She held out a hand and gripped Paco's arm.

"Are you okay?" he said.

"I…I think so. I…."

"I'm so sorry."

"I know. I think…."

"You need a doctor?"

"No, I…" Mary rolled over on her side. "Let me just test…. Let me…."
Paco helped her to her feet.

"Wish you'd watch where you're going."

She was very wobbly, and Paco worried that she would fall again. "Yes, ma'am. I'm sorry. I…." He helped her steady herself at the wall, and there they both looked out to sea.

—

Paco ordered an Uber. The driver—"Bruno, from Brazil, *senhora*!"—had seemed surprised by Mary's appearance as he had slowed to pick them up. Or perhaps more accurately, he was surprised that Mary was in Paco's company, whose mode of dress was significantly more adventuresome than was the nun's. His way over-sized T-shirt advertised the Golden State Warriors. The baseball cap, worn backwards just now, advertised some obscure software product, the name of which no doubt had meaning for someone. He had found his Levis on a Goodwill rack, having wandered into the Mission Street store one day with Yo a few months earlier. He had guarded his skateboard carefully as he tried on pants. The pair he liked fit him in the way other young guys' Levis fitted them, the waist a few inches down his butt and barely held up by the belt he wore. A liberal stretch of his red- and black-checked undershorts showed above the belt. The T-shirt covered up most of this, except when Paco took up the bottom of it to wipe sweat from his face. His black curls cascaded in every direction.

Yo had wanted to shoplift the pants, and Paco laughed at the idea, for which Yo accused him of being "way dumb, man." But unlike Yo, Paco had noted the large black man, with an ID badge that read "Miles," who seemed to be following the two boys around the store, and decided it would be better if he paid. Once they arrived at the cashier, Paco saw that the black man was now standing at the front door of the store, as though wishing to assure himself that Paco and Yo had indeed made the purchase. And in fact he inspected Paco's bag and demanded the sales slip, even though Paco knew that he had witnessed the entire transaction.

"Nice skateboard, man," Miles muttered.

Mary's clothing was far quieter. A white long-sleeved blouse and a dark blue wool skirt. A dark blue wool sweater. Comfortable black walking shoes with laces. Her hair was curled and gray. She knew she did not have a lot of style. But what nuns do? she often asked herself. She had worn her hair the same since she had made her formal vows with the Maryknolls in 1975. Her style existed in her religious name, Mary Inocencia, which she loved, and in the unruly emotions that still coursed through her, back and forth: joyous, rough, embattled, serene, sorrowful, and rage-filled, especially after she had been escorted back to the Monrovia convent from El Salvador, driven almost mad by the murders.

"You're going to...where is it?" Bruno checked his cellphone. "Turk Street?"

"Yes, Bruno," Mary said. "Just up from Lone Mountain College."

"Okay." He wheeled through traffic for a while. "You two related?"

"No." Mary glanced toward Paco who, still embarrassed by his poor handling of the skateboard, was tending to his wounds. Except for a bruise and a slight scrape on one arm, she was not herself hurt, and she had noted his manners that, despite his dress (and the skateboard,) had been so kindly.

"I thought maybe you were his grandmother." Bruno smiled. His reflection was cut off at the bottom of his forehead by the top of the rear-view mirror.

"Oh, no. We just met...sort of." Mary turned to Paco. "What's your name?"

"Paco," Paco whispered.

"*¿Mexicano?*"

Now, for the first time, Paco himself smiled. "I was born in El Salvador."

"*¿Salvadoreño?*"

"Yeah. You know it?"

"Oh..." Mary looked away, frowning. "I lived there for a few years."

Paco removed his palm from his bloodied elbow and checked out the wound. It would be okay, he decided. "You did?"

"Yes, I..."

"You speak Spanish?"

"I do."

"What were you doing there?"

Mary frowned once more. Her brow knitted as she looked away. She leaned her elbow on the door rest and gazed out the window.

"Maybe none of my business," Paco said.

"Oh, no, Paco, I…." She took in a breath and, for the moment, could not speak. "When did you and your parents come here?"

Paco fingered one of the wheels on his skateboard, on end between his legs. "They…well, they…." He went silent.

Bruno had been listening to the conversation. He now glanced at Paco in the rearview mirror.

"They what?" she said.

"They never made it."

Mary's stomach tightened. *Maura,* she thought. *Romina.* She too, just now, could not speak. She waited. Paco noticed her shyness, as, apparently, did Bruno. Neither attempted to divert her from it, although both clearly wished to do so.

She had not turned her eyes toward Paco. She stared out the window, away from him. He waited. The car continued, Paco and Bruno both respecting the suddenness of what seemed, to Paco at least, to be…well, terror.

"They didn't make it?"

"They died in the desert," Paco said. "They were killed by the *coyotes* they had paid to bring them across."

"How do you know that, Paco?"

"My grandmother told me."

—

Mary invited Paco into the retired nuns' home. She had assured the boy that she had no injuries, that she was blessed and so on. But he had insisted—rather gracefully, she thought—that he accompany her to the door. When they had first collided, she had expected Paco to stand up, dust himself off, and skateboard into the distance. She had seen a lot of skateboarders, most of whom were pretty rude in their demeanor: disrespectful, noisy, often obscene and on the whole thoughtless. But Paco's behavior after their run-in surprised her. He continued being concerned, despite the violent initiation of their acquaintance. Skateboarders weren't supposed to be that way.

"Will you come in for a cup of tea?" Mary said.

Paco shrugged and began turning away.

"We won't hurt you." Mary wished for more conversation with Paco because of the news about his parents. "Do you like tea?"

"My grandmother makes me tea every time I visit her."

"Where is she?"

"Out on Forty-second Avenue. You know, toward the beach." Paco slung the skateboard beneath his right arm and looked past Mary as she opened the front door to the nuns' home.

"You're Catholic, I'll bet," Mary said.

He smiled. A sigh came from him. He didn't answer, rather looked through the entry hall. Sister Rebecca Catherine, who was ninety-six, sat on a couch in the living room. Rebecca Catherine didn't speak. Indeed, she hadn't for fifteen years.

"I *was* a Catholic" Paco said.

"But you gave it up?"

"Yes, Sister, after I got into junior high?"

"Why?"

Paco entered the building. Sister Rebecca Catherine seemed to notice him, although he could not be sure.

"It wasn't…. It just wasn't—"

"For you," Mary said.

"Yes, Sister."

Mary nodded. She didn't object. The Church hadn't been for her either for the few years after her return from El Salvador, and she suspected the reason for her heart's emptiness back then was way more mortally compelling than anything this nice boy would understand, despite what had happened to his parents.

Mary made tea in the kitchen that adjoined the dining room of the sisters' home. She brought the pot and two cups on saucers into the living room. Paco had been sitting near Sister Rebecca Catherine. Neither had attempted speech: Paco because he had never been in such a place before, and worried that his appearance and behavior would somehow, unbeknownst to him, be way out of line; Sister Rebecca Catherine because she was continuously deluged by silence.

"Will Sister…Sister…?" He gestured toward the old nun.

"No." Mary paid little attention to Rebecca Catherine. Not from indifference. She simply knew that the nun had no idea where she was or who was with her. Words were beyond her, although Mary remembered how humorously chatty and affectionate she had been before the Alzheimer's had, so to speak, wiped the slate clean for her.

Mary sat down and, bringing the rim of the cup to her lips, pondered the calm with which Paco had told her what had happened to his mother and father. There were few details beyond the one that they had perished in the desert. Mary felt there was no need for such details. The boy and his grandmother now had only themselves, and the brevity of Paco's explanation personified for the nun the immediacy and totality that she knew violent death can represent, even to those who have not actually witnessed that death.

"What'd you do in El Salvador, Sister?" Paco leaned the skateboard against the end table and took up the cup of tea. He sipped from it. Mary's shoulders wavered, and for Paco her eyes became almost stolid with the wish *not* to reply.

After a long moment, Paco replaced the cup and saucer on the table. He worried that he was asking the most wrong question that he ever could. He took in a breath and decided that he should excuse himself. Mary seemed afraid to respond to him. She had paled, and he saw how tightly her fingers were intertwined with each other, how her hands gathered like a tight ball of twisted wire on her lap.

He reached for his skateboard. "Sister, maybe I should—"

"Paco. *¡No me abandones!*"

The urgency in her voice checked him. He sat back.

"Please." Mary's lips had tightened. She studied her hands. "Please. I want to tell you a story."

The skateboard slid to the floor, wheels up. Paco would have taken it up again had he not recognized Mary's descent into sorrow.

—

"Mary, you'd better come with me," Romina said. "Something terrible has happened."

Sister Romina was in charge of the Maryknoll teaching mission in San Salvador. A Mexican, she had once told Mary that she had wanted to be a nun since she was six. She grew up in the orphanage at the *Hospicio Cabañas* in Guadalajara, which had been founded by the Church in 1791. She did not know who her parents were.

What had overwhelmed her when she was a little girl was the painting Jose Clemente Orozco had done of a man on fire ascending into heaven. He is located in the grand nave that rises above the enormous *Hospicio* church ceiling, the nave supported by a dozen curved vaults. It is a huge bubble-like hole, the inside of which is like a perfectly round, hollowed-out cloud. The man, who is ascending through space far, far above, occupies almost all the room inside the cupola. He is without clothing, something about which all the children at one time or another would nudge each other and laugh. He is foreshortened from his feet to the top of his head, the farthest extent of his outstretched, ascending body. His musculature surges within him. He is surrounded on all sides by the flames of hell. He and the fire are circled by the outstretched arms of two sinister men, extended around the entire figure of the man in flames, and joined at each other's hands. They are gray-black, devils maybe, of murderous intent and certainly uncompromising silence. As a child, Romina had always been frightened by them because they appeared to be like obdurate prison guards, keeping anyone away who would save the burning man from exploding into ash and seared flesh.

"The *most* fun for us was carrying the little hand mirrors around," Romina had once told Mary. "For the tourists. They had to lean way back to see the man, and for a lot of them he was, well, too menacing. You know, on fire, as though hell were tossing him out." She smiled. "Orozco was cruel that way, I guess. I even saw a few tourists faint. Those older Catholic ones that feel the man is an angel or something, and is real, but is condemned. The sight of him so far above, carried up by the flames of perdition? It was too much for them. Condemned to heaven, maybe! But we children had those mirrors, which we gave to the tourists for a *peso* or two. That way, all they had to do was look down into the mirror, so that they could see up." She covered her lips with a closed hand. "That was funny when we were six. We laughed about it in the dormitory at night."

"Did the tourists talk to you?"

"Sometimes. The ones who could speak Spanish. But even then, I knew they felt sorry for us orphans, which I didn't like." Romina shrugged, a sad smile crossing her lips. "We didn't even have shoes, Mary…but we *did* have the man of fire." Adjusting the buttons of her blouse, Romina fingered the rosary she had pulled from the pocket of her skirt. "We had him all day and all night, and they only had him for a couple minutes during visiting hours, looking into the mirrors." She kissed the crucifix and replaced the rosary in the pocket. "God forgive me, Sister. I shouldn't have, but I liked it that they didn't have the flames. They did have shoes, which we didn't. But we didn't care about that."

But now, Romina couldn't smile. It was terrible news that she had, which she could barely express, and Mary took Romina's hand.

Romina had begun quivering. Anguish flowed from her. "Something… something…." She wept, and was clearly attempting to control herself, though unsuccessfully. Mary waited. The tears continued.

"I'll drive," Mary said. "Where are we going?"

"The U.S. embassy."

Mary took up a box of Kleenex and handed it to Romina. "But what happened?"

Romina put on a jacket. "I'm not sure."

"Please, Sister. What happened?"

"I don't know. We may have to—"

"What?"

Romina sat down and leaned forward as she brought her open hands to her face. Squashed tears ran down the backs of her hands, coming ashore on the cuffs of her white blouse.

Mary knelt before her and took her by the shoulders. "Sister."

"We've lost them," Romina muttered.

"Lost? What do you mean?"

Romina sat up. Her face was swollen, her normally lovely brown skin, which had no blemish of any kind, now grey and puffed. "They told us they've been killed, Mary."

"Who told you?"

"Oh, Mary…."

"Who was killed?"

—

As they entered the embassy, the two women were met by an American official, dressed in a dark blue suit and black necktie. "Good morning, ladies. I'm Smith Barnes."

He had the bland inexpressiveness so popular among State Department officers. Everything knowable. Everything understood. Mary recognized the Protestant joylessness in him, with its kindly-seeming composure and obdurate resistance to emotional outburst.

Romina's face was now actually sallow with worry. She could not even speak.

"Why are we here?" Mary said. "What has happened?"

Smith motioned the women up a hallway and escorted them into an empty room. He indicated a conference table, at which they sat down.

"I'm sorry to tell you that four of your companions were killed last night."

"Companions," Mary said.

"Yes, uh…. Forgive me for not knowing the terminology. Four…."

Mary reached to Romina's left and put an arm around her shoulders. Romina, aghast, could not speak.

"'Nuns' is the word you want," Mary said.

"Yes, Sister, thank you." Smith remained concerned-looking, although without any actual change in his demeanor. "They were followed from the airport after a plane came in from the U.S. last night. Two nuns met by two other nuns?"

"No," Romina whispered.

"Yes, Sister. And they all were killed."

"But who did it?"

Smith shrugged. "We don't know. We only know where they are." He reached aside for a manila folder and opened it. "By the side of a dirt road, outside a little *pueblo*."

"A dirt road?" Romina said.

"Yes, Sister."

"And not alive."

"No, Sister."

Now Mary lowered her head.

"In a common grave," Smith said.

Mary felt denial take hold of her heart. "All of them together?"

"Yes, Sister."

She grimaced. "In coffins?"

Smith took in a breath and lowered his head. "No, Sister." He closed the folder. "The villagers told their priest about it, and he notified the bishop, who notified us, and…."

Mary waited and noted that for the first time in the conversation the embassy officer was at a loss for…indeed was stricken for…words.

"What is it, Mr. Barnes?"

"We're going out there this morning, and we need you and Sister Romina to come with us."

"Oh!" Romina slumped against Mary, who held her close.

"We asked them to hold off on…exhuming them," Smith said.

Romina crumpled in her chair. Her bones seemed to Mary to have collapsed.

"Until someone from the Maryknolls could be there to identify them."

A pair of embassy station wagons brought the Americans out from San Salvador, and up a narrow dirt road bordered on both sides by scrub forest. The trees reminded Mary of sticks with shamed leaves. They rounded a curve, and far ahead on the left, Mary saw a crowd of Salvadoreans…farmers…standing around some sort of large object. A number of others stood among the farmers, all with cameras; *gringos, latinos*, and others. As the station wagons came to a halt near them, Mary saw that the object was simply a pile of dirt to the side of a large rectangular hole in the earth, about a foot deep. The hole was a yard or two from the side of the road.

The farmers stood back. A few of them recognized Mary and Romina. As Smith and the nuns approached the hole, he gestured to a policeman who was in charge of the exhumation, and told him to continue.

A few of the farmers went down on their knees and dug with their hands at the loose, dry dirt in the hole. Camera shutters clicked and buzzed, exposure after exposure. One of the photographers told Mary in English that she was in the way. Mary stood her ground. She felt she was needed, so that she could make a strict examination of what was being done, to describe to the other sisters what she and Romina had seen.

"Move, lady, would you?"

She saw in the hole an exposed bare foot in a leather *huarache*, filthy, and the cuff of a pair of soiled pants.

"Lady, would you—"

Mary turned. The photographer was a young, bearded American with shaggy hair. Mary knew the type. A pushy journalist.

"Can't you see I gotta get this?" he said.

Pugnacious....

"Leave us alone," Mary said.

Other cameras, dozens of them, were snapping, clicking, roistering and insistent.

"Look." The photographer put out a hand to move Mary aside. "Move outta the way."

She hit him, a quick slap to his temple. "Do not touch me." She gestured toward Romina. "Do not touch her."

"Lady."

She pointed to the hole. "These women are nuns. We are Maryknolls. They are close friends of ours."

The photographer stepped back and moved to the side. "I'm sorry. I...."

It was an attempted apology, which failed. He did not care. Clear of Mary, he dropped to one knee, raised the Nikon to his face, and started shooting.

The men continued digging for several minutes until one entire body was revealed: a young woman clothed in pants and a work-shirt.

"Sister Maura," Romina whimpered.

They dragged her from the hole by her feet, two or three yards from it. Her arms flailed above her head, their movement throwing up small clouds of dust. Maura and her clothing, and especially her hair, were caked with red and yellow dirt. Clots of the dirt were held together by blood, like carmine mud.

Mary identified her for Smith, who took notes: who Maura was, a description of her body, the condition it was in, his impressions of what may have happened. He too had a camera, and took a full portrait of Maura, which offended Mary. The farmers continued digging and, after an hour and a half, had dragged out the three remaining bodies. All had clearly been beaten before they were killed. Sickened and faint, Romina had had to return to one of the station wagons after Maura had been unearthed. Mary stood next to Smith as each of the others was hauled from the hole and dragged away from it. Their bodies left rough trails in the dirt. Mary identified each one for the embassy officer, even as her heart battled with itself as though it too were about to be assassinated.

—

Paco sat silently. The story…he almost could not bear the story. Mary did not weep, although Paco thought she had the right to. But she remained in obdurate calm.

"My grandmother told me about them," he said.

Mary nodded, once.

"It was kind of famous, wasn't it?" Paco said.

She kept her head down. "Did your grandmother tell you who did it?"

Paco now lowered his head. "She did. It was the army."

"That's right. They thought we were some sort of terrorists or something."

"Yes, Sister."

"Nuns!" Mary took in a breath. "Beaten, and then shot." She glanced toward Paco. "And each one of them was raped."

"I know, Sister. My grandmother told me that, too."

Mary remained silent. Finally, Paco stood up. He approached the chair on which Mary sat and leaned forward, low. He took her hands into his. She gasped, and reached out to embrace him.

"Paco."

—

Paco walked Mary and Edwina up the sidewalk, by the sea wall. He had left his skateboard in his room in Spanishtown. It was a gray day with insistent, although kindly, cold winds. They stopped for a moment by the wall. The beach that extends from it is so large that even when it is crowded, the strollers and surfers appear miniscule. Far away, at the edge of the shore break, a few dogs, that appeared more like scurrying insects, ran into the waters and hurried from them.

"I've prayed for Simón and Rosa ever since," Edwina said.

Mary kept her eyes on the shore break. "Has anybody ever answered?"

"From heaven, you mean?"

"I guess so," Mary said.

"Someone in charge, you mean?"

"Yes."

"Well…." Edwina too surveyed the ocean. It was varying shades of immense gray, dark swells littered with white glare from the sun-struck cloud cover. The surf powered in with the sound of huge, distant machinery. "My son Simón answers. Poor Rosa does." The muscles in her jaw flexed. "But that's all."

"Is it enough for you?"

Edwina let out a breath. She reached up to tousle Paco's hair. "And Paco answers."

The boy smiled, embarrassed.

"I wish I had answers," Mary said. "From someone." She had prayed just this morning, although she knew that those prayers would get the same answer that all the others she had offered, for the repose of Maura's soul and those of her companions, had always gotten. No celestial figure…not Saint Francis of Assisi, not Mother Mary, not Sister Inez de La Cruz, not Mother Teresa…none had ever answered. She had given up even trying The Holy Trinity.

Mary's Catholicism seemed to rise up before her now, as though it were an actual glorious object. But it also appeared decrepit and barely used. Instead, she looked out at the Pacific. It was enormous and, in the end, meaningless to any resolution of the very specific rage she had felt since the morning of the exhumation. But at least the ocean, when the sun shone without interference, was blue, as it had always been. It warmed her heart. It caressed her. None of those nuns had been caressed. All had been obliterated. It could be that none of their souls had been saved in any way, if the unappeasable silence that was the answer to Mary's prayers was to be the kind of salvation the nuns were to enjoy. Such a fate was unbearable for Mary, and she looked to the sea, hoping for the same kind of peace that it had given her as a little girl.

I SO TIRE OF YOU, FITZ, YOU AND YOUR TROUBLES

Fitz's offices were in San Francisco, and his movies were mostly shot there. He felt the city, so situated on its hills that streets often become drop-offs or sheer ascensions, provides a kind of hilarity that suited his comedies.

Fitz did not do tragedies.

He had begun as a mime, becoming known when he was twenty for his appearances with his girlfriend Clarice in Union Square. They would show up dressed alike in baggy white shirts, suspenders that held up baggy black slacks, and black and white Keds. In full make-up, all-clown white, and black berets, they would imitate passers-by, a talent for which Fitz became particularly known. If a corporate lawyer huffed by on his way to a difficult court appearance, Fitz would display the man's grumbling wish to do harm, the audience laughing as he went. The mock saintliness, his hands clasped, his eyes poised on heaven above, with which he did the occasional priest was particularly well known. Fitz could make a wealthy matron shopping downtown into a haughty stilt. He did skateboarders and rode with the self-important juvenile disdain of the usual boarder, only without a board of his own. He could even crash comically, although what he ran into was invisible. He also did dogs. Pembroke Welsh Corgis were Fitz's favorite because, he felt, they found *him* funny. He always positioned himself behind whomever he was imitating, a few feet back, and his impressions became so well known in San Francisco that people would show up in the square, looking for him and hoping that he would do them. It was a treat to be done by Fitz O'Hanlon.

Now, at forty-two, he had won three academy awards: one for his writing, another for his comic acting; a third for his directing...on two of his seven pictures. He had become a super-star moviemaker in full possession of his talents, "a comic genius," the Golden Globes had dubbed him.

The trouble was that Fitz's genius had recently abandoned him.

How funny can you still be? he asked himself. He had encountered the enemy that all comics face, which is the fall into self-regard. He noticed how he now and then abandoned the search for something new and settled upon something old. When this difficulty had first appeared in his writing, he was able to strike it out, start the piece again, and come up with novelty. But as he had written more and more, that wellspring had been losing its waters…slowly at first, later with a descent into drought.

In Fitz's opinion, the basis for all comedy is personal remorse, and his laughter was the surface cover for his own emotional difficulty. But lately, with all his grand success, he had inadvertently slipped into repetitiveness. In his case, the remorse was still there, but it was way too self-congratulatory, and for that his work had sunk into sameness. Same joke. Same pratfall. Same unhappiness. A tweaking here and there gave it a breath of newness…but in the end, Fitz was becoming warmed over.

This caused a problem that he could not have imagined while doing a Corgi. In those times, he and Clarice had shared whatever money they had gotten after having passed their hats to the crowd. It seemed to her to be working out okay. But, with Fitz's nod from Hollywood, they had split up, much to Clarice's sadness.

"Why can't you learn to be happy?" she had asked him while he was on his way out the door for the last time. "Why me, Fitz?"

"It isn't you. You've been wonderful."

He knew that unhappy men often use this line as they are headed down the front steps. He hopes that maybe his wife or girlfriend…or even his boyfriend, having escaped in tears to the gym…will forgive him once this largesse-filled utterance is made. *It's all my fault!* But in Fitz's case, this was the truth. Clarice wasn't the problem.

She had tried to coax him back. She had herself been truly funny in Union Square and argued that Fitz was ruining a fine comedic partnership. "I can write too, you know," she reminded him. "We're a duo." But Fitz wished to ruin himself, although he would not have been able to spell that out for you. It was there, inside him; not necessarily recognized by him, but there without a doubt.

In any case, now, Fitz was being paid millions by his Hollywood backers, and he felt compelled to renew his creativity entirely every time he sat down at his computer. He had never had to think about it when he was doing a skateboarder. But now, the film crew, the actors, the producers, the money, and the audience were all waiting to see what Fitz O'Hanlon would come up with next. Sadly, it was becoming approximately what it had been before.

Fitz used *Final Draft*, the script-writing program of choice for professionals. It allows the script to arrive in the producers' hands looking perfect, and this is good. The depth of heart in a comedy absolutely has to be there in the writing itself: the verbal exchange that brings grand laughter, the built-in-stages joke sequence, the clever sight gags and so on. In the old days, when original scripts had been written on typewriters or hand-written on crumpled sheets of paper, sometimes scraped upon by run-down erasers, or other times rubbled over with other kinds of stains (catsup, Seagram's), writing blunders could slip into approval, passing by beneath the surface messiness of the script itself.

With *Final Draft*, all that had gone away.

So, Fitz was surprised to receive one day in the mail, over the transom, one of these old-fashioned scripts. He could tell right away that it was typewritten. Its revisions had obviously been made while being sworn at, were done again, were scratched out in pencil or huffed over in pen. He thought someone must be making a joke. And then, when he was able to yank the entire script from its manila envelope, read its title, *Ulysses in Oakland,* and find the name of its author, Dark Róisín Sheehy, he searched the inside of the envelope for the *de rigueur* stamped return envelope.

There was none.

The wastebasket received Dark Róisín's script cleanly, although it was knocked over by the force with which *Ulysses in Oakland* found its rear rim

Just then, Fitz recalled learning of the name Róisín from stories his grandmother Rose had told him, which she had gotten from her grandmother Margaret in the letters Margaret had sent to Rose when she was a little girl.

"My grandma Margaret was an only child, too," Rose had explained to the boy Fitz, "just like me. And she was way back in Galway when I was little and livin' in Chicago. She thought the loneliness of small little Rose growin' up in, well…who knew what kind of terrible place out there in the American woods? She thought I *must* be sufferin', and she always asked about me in the letters she sent my mother."

"Were you suffering?" Fitz asked.

"I was. For her, I mean. Because I never met her, you know."

Rose had made sure that Fitz pronounced the Irish name correctly. He had been sitting next to her on her couch. "It's Ro-shéen, Fitz."

He surveyed the aged envelope his grandmother was holding, the recipient's name and address written on the front. The only knowledge Fitz had of his great-great grandmother Margaret came from what he had been told by Rose, who, all those years in Chicago, had never once laid eyes on Galway Bay. Rose had given her daughter, Fitz's mother, the shoebox that contained all the letters from Margaret that she had been able to save. The paper was now browned and yellowed, dried out like late-Fall leaves, the handwriting, as Rose had so often said of it, neat as a pin. "I love you, Rosie," Margaret had written at the end of most of them. "My own Róisín. You won't forget us back here, will ya?"

So, Fitz recovered Dark Róisín's script from the wastebasket. He noticed the corner of a folded letter sticking out of the manila envelope and discovered it had been written by Clarice. It revealed that Dark Róisín was her boyfriend. Because of the difficulty of Fitz and Clarice's break-up so long ago and the contrition it caused in him now, Fitz opened the script and read it.

Two days later, Dark Róisín Sheehy sat across the desk from Fitz.

"*Are* you Irish?" Fitz said.

He sat back in his leather chair and surveyed the new skyscrapers that surrounded his office building on Howard Street, south of Market. When he had first moved in, this part of San Francisco had been notable for its empty warehouses, vacant lots, and wasteland-like dereliction. His own building, original to the neighborhood in 1896, was made of brick and had four floors. It had survived the 1906 conflagration, the only building on the block to do so. There wasn't a lot to it architecturally.

Now, though, the tech-crowd had invaded the city, and enormous multi-story slabs, gleaming like mirrors high up in the sun, had replaced all that emptiness. *But,* Fitz thought as he watched the crowds of youthful software engineers hurrying up and down the sidewalks outside, noses planted in their iPhones, *this is all just* new *emptiness.* Until a few years ago, sunlight had entered the windows of his office freely. Lately, the continuous shadows cast by these new buildings—invaded only now and then by narrow but brazen sun-glare—darkened the windows so definitively that Fitz had given the gloom various personalities, depending upon the time of day.

Such darkness actually was necessary to his comedy, which was knockabout. Fitz knew well how to pull a laugh from despondency because he had done it so often. He looked to Buster Keaton, Stan Laurel, Jacques Tati and others for inspiration. The tender helplessness with which Charlie Chaplin's tramp so often flirts with Edna Purviance, for instance, comes from deep self-doubt. The audience's affectionate glee is the result.

But the shadows from the tech company skyscrapers could not be blamed for the loss of comic abilities from which Fitz was suffering. Although these new buildings were all demonstrable failures, they were not human. Fitz's particular troubles came from his own failures which, of course, *were* human.

With Clarice, for example.

"No." Róisín pursed his lips. "I was born in Oakland." He described himself as a longshoreman. "I have my union card. But since this got going…" He gestured toward the script. "I've been staying close to home."

"Clarice."

"Yeah. And you know it can still be a little dangerous out there on the docks." Róisín raised his eyebrows, looking for understanding. "At least it was in 1934!"

Fitz caught the reference.

"When the union went out on strike," Róisín said. "My great-uncle Joey Sheehy was in the union, and he got cracked on the head." He grinned. "I been waiting for that to happen to me!"

Fitz's grandfather John O'Hanlon had begun his work on the San Francisco docks too, running messages up and back on the waterfront. He had gone on to found a successful ship chandlery business that Fitz's father had taken over. Solidly anti-union. The business failed as shipping left San Francisco, a demise for which Fitz's father never forgave himself. He died of drink, which was a childhood source, Fitz knew, of the secret to his comedy.

"But I guess I could pass for Irish." Róisín sat up straight and assumed a regal look, his profile held high over his shoulders. "All those Gaels and their sheep." He glanced toward Fitz.

"But Róisín's a girl's name," Fitz said.

"It is." Róisín adjusted himself in his chair.

Most of Fitz's Hollywood contacts dressed in the modern casual manner of the homeless, although his contacts' clothing was at least laundered. The homeless look is what stands for fashion in these times. Ties? Nah. Suits? Only occasionally, and certainly without a tie of any sort. Levis and T-shirts are the norm, with an occasional regular shirt, with buttons and so on. Such a shirt, though, is suspected of being fashion imperialism. Presidential candidates and members of Congress still wear suits, although when campaigning, they too effect the casual sloppiness of the rest of the population. Fitz himself dressed in this way.

"And I went to Oakland High School." Róisín had placed the wool, brimmed cap he wore on his lap. "So, I know the town." His Timberland pants were worn out, the cuffs messily rolled up. His blue denim shirt was clearly wrinkled, noticeable especially in the collar. The shirt was tucked in, although still a mess. He wore an old, stained Levi's jacket, unbuttoned, and had on a pair of Redwing boots, the sort that the guys building all the new skyscrapers in the neighborhood wore: scraped, worn down at the heels, and beat up.

"But do you think James Joyce ever even heard of Oakland?" Fitz said.

Róisín's face accompanied the look of his clothing. It had many wrinkles and the cheeks and forehead were turning gray, although a lighter gray than his hair, which was disheveled…mostly because of his need for a haircut, Fitz concluded. But Róisín had presence…a working-class guy telling management to shove it you-know-where. *This is the kind of guy who stands up on a box, exhorting union mobs to action,* Fitz thought.

"No. So what?" Róisín said.

Fitz discerned in this abrupt response the light of good humor.

"*Ulysses* is about Dublin, right? Which is a dump, or at least was a dump in Joyce's time. And Oakland is still a dump now. So…" Róisín turned to the side in his chair. He stroked his chin with the fingers of his right hand. "So, it's perfect."

"Does anyone who goes to my movies know anything about *Ulysses*?"

"They don't. But because so many of them do go to your movies, you have a fine opportunity to give them a taste." Róisín turned back to face Fitz. "You know, Leopold Bloom wanders around Dublin for that day in *Ulysses*, neighborhood to neighborhood, shop to shop, brothel to whore-house. And most of it is funny."

"You think so?"

"I do." Róisín pointed at the script in Fitz's hands. "Even though what I wrote there is in Oakland, and everyone in it talks in American accents — black accents, Latino accents, Asian accents — the place…" He grinned and leaned forward to examine his shoes. "…the place is perfect for making fun of…just like Dublin was."

Fitz pushed the script aside despite the fact that he too thought it a riot. But it had so many scenes. Six hours long, maybe? Seventy-seven characters. He had to admit, though…it *was* hilarious.

"You wondered about my name," Róisín said. "It's my pen name,"

"So then, your…your—"

"Real name? It's Oren Cadwallader."

"Oren."

"Yeah! My grandfather's name. From Texas." Róisín fiddled with his cap. "The Panhandle."

"What did he do, your grandfather?"

"A cowpoke." Róisín now crossed his legs, and surveyed Fitz with a look of kindly disapproval. He was maybe fifty years old, and his hair, which was also full with benevolent curls, seemed to want to struggle from his skull.

"I know it's a woman's name. But that doesn't matter. I wrote the script for Clarice, see? and she loves it. She told me it was made for you and your…ironic talents." Róisín pronounced the last two words with a kind of searching disdain. "Comedy, see?" Fitz sensed he was being made fun of. "No offense, that business about irony…" Róisín said.

"That's all right."

"…or about talent."

"It's okay. I recognize Clarice's, uh, humor in it." Fitz grinned.

"Maybe so. But she means what she says about what I wrote." Róisín sighed. "She thinks the script's one of a kind. That's why she sent me to you."

"You know what Clarice said to me, don't you? The day she left."

"Sorry. She told me it was you who left."

The chairback suddenly felt as though it were jabbing at Fitz.

Róisín sat forward. "She told me…what was it?" He pondered the thought. "'I so tired of Fitz, him and his troubles.'"

"She did say that, yes. To me, too." Fitz grumbled. "And you want me to option this script, having told me that?"

A softness in Róisín's gaze eased the discomfort of the moment. He shrugged, and with that motion seemed to be apologizing. "I do, yes." He took up his cap again and turned it about by its sweatband, examining its insides. "I do."

There would have to be all kinds of edits, every sort of change in the thing. It sprawled and lurched. It didn't seem to know what it wanted. It went off on side-jolts that maybe couldn't even be filmed at all. But it was the funniest script Fitz had ever read. He actually wished he had written it himself.

"Where does your comedy come from?" he asked.

Róisín fixed Fitz with a glance that seemed amazed.

"Is it emotional deprivation?"

"What?"

"Sadness? Anger?"

"Where's it come from? I don't know where it comes from." Róisín reached forward and took up the script, to thumb through it. "Comedy's funny. What else do you want?"

"Fitz's Tomb" was what Fitz called it. He couldn't quantify it as something knowable…or traceable. He only knew he had always been buried in it. His childhood had been spent causing laughter for everyone. Grandparents, aunts, uncles, even his parents had always loved having him around. The moms of his school pals at Saints Peter and Paul asked their kids to bring Fitz over for cookies and milk. Even Father Ginestera, the principal when Fitz was a pupil there, was able to put aside his snarls when he came across Fitz in the school hallways. The priest, who never smiled, did smile when Fitz came into view.

But there were times when Fitz was knocked into black self-rebuttal. He didn't know why he had to be so gloomy…but he was. His mother noticed it and could tell that one of these moments had arrived when she would find Fitz in bed, refusing to get up. He would turn away and pull the pillow over his head. She decided that leaving him alone was the best way to get him to get funny again, which he always did.

He felt in those moments he was a piece of dark waste, and he still suffered from them. They were somehow connected, he had concluded, to his general demeanor of happy riot. When he wasn't secluded and silent, he couldn't hold himself back. People loved Fitz then, and he decided not to worry about the moments when he was so obviously disembodied from himself. They would go away soon enough, and he would get out of bed in order to make everyone laugh again. He always assured himself. He *would* get out of bed.

Fitz called Clarice later that afternoon.

"You want to take me to lunch?" she asked.

"Yes. It's this script."

"Oren's."

"Uh…well, Dark Róisín's."

For a moment, Fitz could hear only Clarice's chuckling. "It's a pen name."

"I know. I know."

They met at the farmer's market the following Saturday, outside The Ferry Building. As usual, the crowd wandered about in a state of amused elation, pleased to be surrounded by such color and humorous talk. It is the good-natured purity of the fruits and vegetables that makes this market so enjoyable. Fitz and Clarice had frequented it early every Saturday morning when they were together. They would later leave the things they had bought in their car in the garage below Union Square. Because they were not yet made up at the market and were out of costume, they were able to shop without being recognized.

"It's nice to see you, Fitz," Clarice said.

"You, too."

They embraced. Tentatively.

Clarice d'Angelo was still acting in small theater venues. She had little money, while Fitz had made all his after their breakup. The one thing that had been overly successful in her Union Square make-up was its covering up of her singular New York Italian beauty. She had gotten it, she said, from her mother, who remained—ever complaining—in Manhattan, escaped from by Clarice when she had come to the west coast to go to university at Berkeley. By way of explanation, Clarice had told Fitz that, per capita, there are more psychiatrists in New York City than any other city in the U.S. "And do they need them!" Clarice dressed with style, knowing how to shop at used-clothing stores and in flea markets. Her comedy had always been different from her usual demeanor. When not doing their act, she was quiet, stunning, and often saddened by all the things her mother had said to her in her childhood. Clarice's skin, of Mediterranean soft-glowing grace, was made even more so by her eyes. Fitz had told her once that those eyes were part of what made her comedy in the square so unusual. "When somebody is arrested by them," he had said, "the fact you're so funny comes as a surprise. Which part does the audience believe: the heaven in those eyes or the laughs?"

Fitz had brought an extra cloth bag with him and handed it to Clarice. "In case you see some carrots you like."

As they walked, they talked.

"What would it be like, working with Róisín," Fitz said.

Clarice looked over the small gatherings of cilantro on the stand before her. Fitz had often complimented the *chimichurri* she made, which, although she was no Argentine, he knew was the most famous such addition to meat ever to come from that country.

Clarice lowered her head and caressed the cilantro with her fingers. "You remember when my mother visited me?"

"I do."

Her lips tightened. "We had a barbecue that night…ribs, remember? So delicious. And I made my *chimichurri* for her. I loved cilantro."

"I remember."

"But she thought it tasted bad, and when I asked why, she asked me what were the greens in it? I told her, and she laughed. 'Listen, I heard on the radio the other day that there's no cilantro in Argentina.'" Clarice frowned with the recollection. "'So, this couldn't possibly be *chimichurri*,' she told me. I looked at her as though she were the enemy…which, of course, she was." Fitz could tell how hurt Clarice still was. "My mother doesn't know *anything* about *chimichurri*." Clarice fingered a few of the rubber-banded gatherings of the green resting on the stand before her. "She never did." She shook her head. "My poor, darling cilantro."

She bought a sprig of the green and placed it in her bag. "But working with Róisín? That'd be different. It'd be all right. He's talented."

"Has he ever sold a screenplay?"

"He doesn't know the first thing about it." They turned away from the stand and continued on. "That's where you come in."

The noise from the vegetable and fruit stands, the hawking, and the laughter brightened Clarice's mood. But Fitz worried. "It'll never fly in Los Angeles."

"That's up to you, Fitz."

Fitz was also worried about something else. "How will you and I get along in all this?"

She let out a sigh. Fitz sensed in it the depth of thought she had given to their break-up. "Forgive me, Fitz." Clarice gathered the cloth bag into both hands, cilantro and all. "I *was* tired of you."

"I know."

"And Róisín makes me happy."

"He does?"

"He doesn't mope."

Fitz remained silent.

"He cares for others besides himself."

Fitz lowered his head, leaned forward, and studied the tips of his loafers. On the sidewalk, there were stains from trodden-upon strawberries.

"He's lovely," Clarice said.

The following Monday, Dark Róisín sat once more in Fitz's office.

"We'll take it," Fitz said.

Róisín glowered. Suddenly he gave off a look that conveyed barely escaped surprise. "Yeah, but for how much?"

Fitz's lips lowered at each edge. He shrugged. "A hundred?"

"A hundred bucks? Are you kidding?"

"No. No, Róisín! A hundred thousand."

Róisín was able to bring a halt to the half-accomplished movements of standing and striding for the conference room door. He sat back down. "Say that again."

"One hundred thousand dollars."

A longish silence ensued. Fitz kept his eyes on Róisín, whose elbows were solidly propped upon the arms of the chair. He seemed to be awaiting a disclaimer from Fitz, or laughter. Róisín clearly suspected he was being made fun of.

"But we'd expect to make some changes," Fitz said.

Róisín was flummoxed. "You pay me that, you can do whatever the fuck you want."

"It'll be shorter."

"How much?"

"About fifty percent of what it is now."

"And I'll bet you're—"

"Twenty-five or so characters instead of…" Fitz took up the script. "However many there are here." He dropped the script back to the table. "And I'll tell you what. We'll even keep the title."

"You will?"

"It's terrific. *Ulysses in Oakland*. People will come to see it just to find out what a title like that means."

"I guess so."

"Róisín. Nobody in Oakland knows anything about *Ulysses*…"

"Yeah, I guess."

"…or cares."

"I guess."

"I mean, they don't even know about the *original* Ulysses."

Róisín lowered his head. "Yeah, him, too." His hands hung listlessly from the ends of the armchair's arms.

The three of them worked on the script for two months. There was argument, dismay, sparkling glee, grudging silence, celebratory downing of many glasses of wine, and the sense, despite each's resentment of the others from day to day, and the resultant flows of forgiveness, that the script was getting better. They laughed and laughed and laughed.

The project almost failed when, after Fitz had agreed that it was ready, he called Dark Róisín the next day and said he had thought about it and felt they needed to cut it even more.

Róisín voiced his exhaustion with what they had been through. This new news was too much for him. "Listen, you take this script the way it is now, or I'll toss it out and give you back your hundred thousand."

"Róisín. Hang on."

"I'll go down to Disney, and *they'll* take it."

Fitz laughed, which resulted in long silence from Róisín. *What does he know about Disney?* Fitz thought. And in fact, Róisín had correctly guessed that Fitz felt he was being a fool. But Róisín's declaration actually had unleashed a secret for Fitz. His anguish, which had walked along with him every step since his early boyhood, rose up and jabbed him in the side. It was the worry that, really, there was not much to him, although he had encountered in his work with other people the kind of profane reluctance to change things that Róisín too brought with him. But he had learned that Dark Róisín *could* make changes and *could* put aside the insult that accompanied a suggestion for an edit. His judgment was good. He was open-minded. The script got funnier whenever he agreed to something from Fitz or Clarice. Not from the suggestion; rather from his ability to come up with something better once the suggestion was made.

Fitz, who had been through such difficulties with his own scripts, admired Róisín's lithe touch when such battles broke out. He himself had often stormed from script sessions in a rage because of the suggestions made by some studio executive or producer. It was his conviction that such people aren't funny and can't write. But Róisín was unbothered. He would mutter a few harsh expletives, wander around the room mumbling to himself for a while, scratching his head, and then get back to it.

Clarice, often trying to referee the conversations, herself rewrote several scenes in such ways that the comedy was given a light freshness that didn't always exist in other scenes. The main character, Ulysses Rose, hadn't had a girlfriend until Clarice insisted on one, and she wrote all the dialog for the part. What she wrote reminded Fitz of Clarice herself. Róisín agreed. The two men also agreed that she was the only actress who would understand the part. Clarice had to play it.

She also handled the fellows in L.A. better than Fitz or Dark Róisín.

"Fitz. Come on! Nobody's gonna pay to see this." Harvey Littleman was himself from Manhattan originally, and didn't care for Los Angeles. "I don't like palm trees," he explained. He came from Broadway musicals. "Or beach balls." Fitz felt Harvey knew hardly anything about movies and how they are made, other than his gift for making money from them. He sometimes described film industry people as a waste of his time. "Directors, actors and so on," Harvey would say. But he ran Littleman Films, which was one of the most successful indie film companies in L.A. He had funded and co-produced all three of Fitz's movies.

When Harvey asked what Clarice's role was in this meeting, Fitz explained that she was one of the writers. Clarice, on her phone at the moment, had not noticed the whispering between the two men.

"She's cute," Harvey said.

"Well, that's not—"

"She got a boyfriend?"

Clarice had just then hung up, and the question went unanswered.

Now, Clarice was sitting at a corner of the conference table, at a ninety-degree angle from Harvey. She splayed her hands apart and leaned forward. "Harvey, we saw you laughing a couple minutes ago." The light touch of her voice seemed to disarm Harvey. There was a playfulness in her speech that throughout the meeting had charmed the producer. "We saw how much you were enjoying that scene."

In the script, Ulysses was bantering with himself on a bench on the shore of Oakland's Lake Merritt, about why it was that he couldn't make any money writing code. He was watching a woman named Mollie, who at this point he didn't yet know. But Mollie was flirting with Ulysses. She would be major in the movie, and was the woman whom Clarice would play.

"Me?" Harvey had two or three days of unshaved beard on his face. He was balding, and the skin below his eyes seemed to be sliding from them, like over-saturated mud down a steep slope. He needed to lose a lot of weight, and the hems and haws that preceded each utterance contained a lining of fat.

"Mollie is a real possibility for him," Clarice said. "And you liked that. You liked the way we were setting it up."

"I did?"

"It was obvious." Clarice tapped the script where it lay on the table. "I wrote that scene." She looked to Fitz and Róisín. "Right?" They both nodded. "I know how to make a woman be fun." She cocked her head to the side, a gesture that seemed to delight Harvey. "I know how Ulysses will react."

"Who's gonna play Ulysses?" Harvey said.

Clarice sat back, slouching in her chair. "Fitz!"

Harvey glowered. "You mean I got to pay him for that too?"

Clarice had structured her conversation with Harvey in such a way that he felt included on her defense of the scene. He was clearly charmed by Clarice's clear appreciation of his fine, thoughtful taste.

"I know how men react," she said. She offered him a smile.

Later, after Harvey left the conference room — "Yeah, we'll do it. Listen, I got a Zoom conference." — Clarice stood and raised a fist. "Did you hear that?" Fitz and Róisín were busy shaking each other's hand. But Clarice insisted they pay attention to her. "Did you two hear that?" She so grinned that Fitz was taken back to the moments when they worked together, when, after she removed her makeup, he would actually sigh with appreciation of how electrifying she was. "You can manipulate a man like him without even trying," Clarice said. And she was *so* funny! "A sap like that." She stuffed the script into her shoulder bag. "Let's get outta here."

Fitz *was* falling in love again. He had not left Clarice because of the Hollywood breakthrough. Money had not been part of the breakup. Only now, though, when they were working together again, did he finally real-ize what she had brought to their happiness. Fitz had grown convinced that he was the source of all the comedy in Union Square. It was he who people came to the square to see, and he to whom Hollywood had come. He had not realized then that Clarice was the force that most successfully brought him from his anger and sadness, who enabled him to strut around as a clown once more and knock the audience out. She was an opera fan, and when she had taken him to standing room at the San Francisco Opera to see *Pagliacci*, Fitz had recognized himself. In the famous scene in which Canio the clown puts on his makeup and sings "Vesti la giubba," Fitz had recalled looking at himself in the Union Square garage men's room every Saturday, putting on his makeup. The aria had caused him to weep, even as he had not understood the lyrics. Clarice had had to comfort him on the way home from the opera house. But Fitz knew what Canio was thinking. To make sure, he looked up a translation of the aria. *"Laugh, clown,/at your broken love!"*

Now, Fitz realized that he had indeed been nuts to abandon the love he and Clarice had had.

He sought Clarice's forgiveness. They were sitting on the back porch of his house on Russian Hill. Róisín was inside looking over the script. The view of the Golden Gate in the distance had always made Fitz think of post cards. As a kid, he had noticed the actual bridge now and then. But what he really liked were post cards of it, the kind he collected. The Empire State Building. Mount Rushmore. The post cards were quick, entertaining, and instantaneous…the way Fitz himself was.

He noticed in this moment, though, how Clarice was studying the view. He recalled how she had so often asked him to wait as she was explaining some comic possibility. Fitz would have taken the idea up immediately and begun riffing on the possibilities. But Clarice had the long view in mind. This wasn't just a patter of one-liners. "I'm making up a scene, Fitz. Wait. Give me a moment." He had sometimes actually resented Clarice's wish for time. Development took time and was not itself funny. The wisecrack was funny, and time wasn't.

"Clarice, I've enjoyed what we're doing now."

She remained silent, observing the bridge. But she was listening.

"Working again like this."

She looked down at her hands, folded together on her lap.

"I hope you'll—"

"I can't, Fitz."

He glanced toward her and noticed her tightened lips.

"I love Róisín, and love what he's written."

"But—"

"Keep your eyes on what we're doing, Fitz."

"But, Clarice."

"Thank you, Fitz. But this is more important."

"You don't think we could—"

"No, I don't."

Fitz attempted gathering himself.

"Thank you." Clarice looked again toward the bridge. There were no clouds. The air was bright. "It's nice of you," she said. "But this…what we have going now…is very important."

"But—"

"If you want to forgive yourself, Fitz, help Róisín make his movie."

Dark Róisín and Clarice were engaged to be married three months later, the week after *Ulysses in Oakland* was green-lighted. They invited friends to a party at Tosca, where Fitz offered a toast. It was only a little half-hearted, the toast; indeed, he meant it. He understood the rules and Clarice's justification of them. Now forty, Clarice still looked like she was twenty. For the party, she wore a deep purple ankle-length silk dress that would have been perfect on Lauren Bacall. It was pretty stunning on Clarice d'Angelo, and she loved the large bouquet of roses that Róisín had ordered for her. The bouquet was a love-surging secret, the surprise of which Clarice adored. It also happened that Disney had made an offer to Harvey for a joint production of *Ulysses in Oakland*. Dark Róisín was considering a resultant writing offer from Littleman Films for another project. Clarice, a relative unknown in the movies, had nonetheless just appeared in a fashion shoot for *Paris Vogue* and had been asked to write and direct a comedy for Netflix.

Fitz was on a new project as well. His muse had begun its gradual return to him the day he had tossed *Ulysses in Oakland* into his waste-paper basket. Clarice was worried about this new project, while Fitz himself was grateful for it. Yes, it was about a couple of young mimes making fun of people in Union Square and falling in love. But it was something he had never written about, and it was erupting from him. It was brand new.

PARKER AND BUDDY

P arker sat in the front row of Grace Cathedral, not much enjoying the priest's encomiums. It was true that his mother, April Evans, had been one of the great jazz singers. Her many recordings alone would confirm it. But it was her manner on stage and the particular timbre that singing before a crowd gave to her voice that made going to a club, buying the expensive tickets, and enjoying the overpriced drinks worth everything from the moment she stepped onto the stand. Joy was mixed with grief in her singing, depending on the lyrics and, more important, the arrangements she had written for each of the songs. She was a natural musician who had gotten her training in little Upper Grant Avenue dumps when she was first trying to sing professionally, to the stands of important San Francisco clubs like Keystone Korner, where she made her first live recording as a twenty-five year old, and then on to New York, Paris, Tokyo, et. al.

Parker himself had loved his mother's voice, even as her travel schedule so often put him in the hands of others for weeks at a time. The *filipina* Jocelyn until he was seven, and then the *mexicanas* Porfíria and María Luz through his high school years. He cared for these women; but even more, he cared about his mother's absences. He missed her. When she was at home, though, she put most of her music aside in order to play with her little boy, escort him to school, cook things that he especially liked… eventually touting his beginnings as a journalist at Galileo High School. He wrote mostly about music. Parker became special to a lot of musicians because his mother had educated him about the music itself. He could read charts and knew about performance and the other struggles that you have to go through to have any kind of authority in front of an audience. Improvisation itself. But also handling the guys in the band, the business of it all, the travel arrangements, the troubles getting paid. Etc.

"Your mother tell you all this, man?" he was once asked by the blues singer Charles Brown just a year before Brown's death. Parker, a junior in high school, showed up for the interview at Brown's home in Oakland, to be asked by the singer, with his famous smile, if Parker had been born just that week. Brown clapped Parker on the back as the young man passed through the front door. "Just a kid!" But Brown was a fan of April Evans's work, so that Parker had enough of an opening to be tolerated by the great man, and the interview went well. "You can come back whenever you want, child," Brown said as Parker made his way down the hallway toward the front door.

One of Parker's special memories was that of watching his mother advise the members of the various bands that had backed her. Usually, they were made up of four or five musicians, and April always ran the show. This was entertaining for Parker because the musicians were for the most part men, and thus sometimes frustrated that they were backing up a woman—"You kiddin'?"—who also had the balls—"You hear what she said to me?"—to write all the charts. It happened that she was white, which was also a problem for some of her sidemen. These whisperings among the musicians had to remain close to the vest, though, because if April heard them, or heard of them, you were gone. Parker, sitting on a chair at the empty Great American Music Hall on a random afternoon, a glass of ginger ale before him at the table, his backpack on the floor next to him and a junior high school homework assignment spread out on the barren bar table before him, enjoyed watching the musicians' occasional miffed silence during rehearsals. Artistically, April was way on the edge. It was clear, always, that she was inventing. Some of these musicians would nonetheless dismiss her *because* she so knew what she was doing. If April heard about that, you were *especially* soon gone. Parker now and then even informed on those guys who were unhappy. He didn't care. Musicians who complained were just complainers, and Parker, who loved his mother, also knew well what she could do.

Few had April Evans's improvisational chops. Also, for every disgruntled piano player, there were others she could call on. The only stipulation was that the excellence of each's playing had to be matched with the good judgment not to cross April musically. There were enough such players to go around, so her ultimate backup guys were terrific, and usually a lot of fun.

But now, April was in her coffin on the altar at Grace Cathedral. It was an open coffin, and he could see the clear line of her profile where it rose from the white satin pillow on which her head rested. Parker, now forty, held to the cotton handkerchief he had brought from his jacket pocket. The dark brown skin below his eyes shined with the residue of tears that the handkerchief had not been able to catch. His glasses, which reminded people of Dizzy Gillespie's, had sometimes fogged up, so that Parker had to remove them a few times during the ceremony. The frames were thick and black and gave to his face the kind of professorial authority that Dizzy's had had. Parker had a more serious personality than the great trumpeter's, something he felt enhanced his credibility for the musicians about whom he wrote. They were often intimidated by writers, feeling that they had to get pontifical when being interviewed. Parker's personal kindness included the ability to put musicians at ease, particularly as it grew clear to them that he too knew what he was doing.

April had died on tour, in Manhattan, a heart attack. Parker, traveling with her at the time, had had to deal with the police officers and medical people. The coroner guy. The Birdland people. The woman from the *New York Times*. They were all of them kind. Even the cops were kind, despite the fact that at first they concluded Parker was just another black man. Their kindness quotient rose once they understood that the deceased was his mother, whom they could not deny was white.

The simple act of answering their questions, which were routine, cluttered Parker's heart with resentment. He understood what these people had to do. He did sympathize with the reasons for their questions. But it was not until the airplane trip home that Parker could begin actually to mourn his mother. It began in the moment he broke the news to his mother's secretary Marvin, a gay man who had been working for her for many years. Marvin's need to sit down the moment he got the news from Parker sounded, over the phone, like a muffled crash, as though several packages had dropped to the floor. Parker waited, wishing to ask Marvin if he were okay. He remained silent because he heard Marvin's continued weeping. Marvin attempted apologies but could not make it through them. Parker listened in silence. He had known Marvin since he was sixteen.

The crowd left Grace Cathedral, many of them pausing on the steps to wait for Parker. He greeted these, accepting their hugs and sentiments. Most declared that they would be attending the memorial concert at the SFJazz main hall the following week. Parker had personally invited a number of musicians who were not on tour somewhere. All had gladly accepted. The crowd dispersed from the steps, leaving Parker to speak with stragglers.

An old man stood to the side of the labyrinth that is imprinted on the upper plaza before the cathedral. The labyrinth itself provides a kind of thoughtful path-seeking to anyone who wishes to walk it, even those who may have few if any Episcopalian sentiments. Around the outside, it forms a circle, and you follow its many pathways inside, sometimes encountering a dead end, other times flowing through a corner that leads to another and then, maybe, sometimes, another. There is contemplative grace in the laby-rinth. Even when you walk into a blocked corner, you can take advantage of the moment to question why such a stop may be a good thing. You turn back, pleased with fresh direction.

Thoughtfulness and quiet, back and forth, up and around.

He was a very thin, very black man. A black business suit, white shirt, and neat silk necktie, properly tied and without wrinkles where it lay against the front of the shirt. A folded overcoat over his left arm. His black leather shoes had not one scuff. He even wore a fedora, of the sort you can see in photos of Martin Luther King Jr. as a young man. Parker imagined that, suddenly, he had been transported into the early Civil Rights movement, and that this man—a playwright, an activist A.M.E. pastor, an historian of black culture—was an acquaintance of James Baldwin (his editor, maybe) or of the recently assassinated Malcolm X.

"Parker?"

He approached Parker with an air of shy rectitude, buttoning and un-buttoning his suit coat.

"Yes."

"You don't know me."

"I'm sorry, sir. I don't."

"So, I hope this isn't too much of a surprise."

Parker extended his hand. "Not a worry. Yes, I'm Parker Evans."

"Named after the great saxophonist."

"Yes, my mother was his biggest fan. She had every record."

"I know that."

"You do?" Parker stood back and surveyed the other man's eyes. They looked into his. A moment of kindness seemed to overtake the introduction. Finally, the man spoke.

"I'm your father."

Parker felt the man's handshake grow even more firm. A shroud of silence fell across both of them.

"My name is Buddy Briggs."

Sympathetic to Parker's sudden trembling, and now smiling as he released the younger man's hand, Buddy suggested they get coffee.

A bit unhinged, Parker made small talk as he escorted Buddy in an Uber to the Caffe Trieste in North Beach. Once a hang-out for the beatnik crowd in the 1950s, it remains one for those few still left alive who totter in all alone. The café is a haven for young poets and others wishing to emulate the notoriety of those originals, so that it is frequently crowded. Silent, angry writers, already poverty stricken—as had been the beatniks themselves—are uniformly armed with ballpoint pens and scratched-up notepads. They use the paper for composing hurried complaints in much-considered, much erased and replaced language. Some of the complaints contain arbitrarily shortened lines so that they pretend to verse. There is also a fair amount of bitter intoning in the café's conversation, usually on political subjects. Republicans are not welcome at The Trieste. But neither are Democrats. It is generally agreed upon that both parties remain in thrall to billionaire corporate crime, and so are not to be trusted. Che Guevara still has high approval here.

Times *have* changed since the 1950s. The laptop computer, for example, has been added to the tools of poetic inquiry, but has done little to improve the general sullenness of the Trieste's clientele.

Parker stood in line with Buddy, who looked through the café, mentioning that it reminded him of a lot of places in The Village in New York.

"Funny that the white avant-garde never changes, isn't it?" he said as they sat down at one of the tables inside the long window that borders Grant Avenue. He unbuttoned his overcoat. He had ordered a muffin and a latte. Placing his fedora on the bench next to him, he fingered the muffin in silence.

"You live in New York?" Parker said. He was trying to maintain some sort of calm. It was difficult because his mother had told him so little about his father. "Oh, Parker, it was a fling," she had said over dinner on his twenty-first birthday. Parker, feeling that this was perhaps the most important birthday ever, sought an explanation from April that was more than just the few detail-less thoughts she had expressed about his paternity since he had been little. "The only thing I really knew was that, once I discovered I had you…you know…" She pointed to her tummy. "I wasn't going to lose you. I just knew that I wanted you. I so wanted you."

"But what about him?" Parker said.

April leaned forward, and Parker recognized the resolve in her wordlessness.

"What *about* him, Mother?"

"I can't…." April shrugged, looking away. "I just can't, Parker. I'm sorry."

The conversation between the two men had been tentative at best. Parker held his breath. He was actually afraid that Buddy would tell him things about April that he did not wish to hear. *Who is this guy? What did he do to her?*

"Did she ever speak about me?" Buddy asked.

Parker shook his head. "All she said was that, if I ever were to meet my father, I should ask *him*."

Buddy nodded. He too held back.

"Are you a musician?"

"I was." Buddy sipped from his coffee. "When I met your mother." He winced with the coffee's bitterness. "I still am, sometimes. But mostly I'm a teacher."

"Where?"

"The Harlem School of The Arts."

"What instrument?"

"The trumpet."

Parker smiled. "Yeah, she liked the trumpet." He now fingered the pastry before him, aware that Buddy was waiting. "Did she like you?"

Buddy winced. Parker knew the question was nervy. Insulting, even. But he did not wish to simply dance around the questions of who his father was, and how it was that *this* fellow was his father. He had been dancing around such questions since the day of his birth.

Buddy swallowed. "The day she told me to leave, she also said that she had once thought she couldn't live without me."

"How did you meet?"

"She had a gig at Bradley's, in The Village, and she needed somebody. I went to the club to play for her, and she liked what I was doing."

"So, she hired you."

"Yes." Buddy took up his latte and sipped from it. He replaced the thick brown ceramic cup on its saucer. His eyes quivered back and forth across it. "And I fell in love with her."

Parker's fingers caressed the brim of his own cup. It had not occurred to him that Buddy could possibly be deeply saddened by the passing of his… what had his mother called it? His fling? So long ago. But he understood now that Buddy was himself overcome with sorrow. Buddy exhaled, a substitute for a moan.

"I did love her." He lifted his eyes to Parker's. "I did." He took in another breath. "She never spoke with you about me?"

Parker shook his head.

"I wouldn't have expected so. I made a terrible mistake, Parker." Buddy sipped again from the coffee. "She was so happy when she learned she had you."

"That's what she told me."

"Oh, she was. It was me, though, Parker. It was me who was unhappy."

"Why?"

Buddy reached for the last of the muffin, which had the task of absorbing his sadness. He crumbled it into small shards that fell to its plate.

"I thought then that it was just some kind of game. I thought we'd just been playin', see?" Buddy pushed the shards together into a small pile. "I'm sure that, for you, that's an insult, Parker."

"It is. But if she couldn't live without you…that's more than just playin'."

"It makes sense that's how you'd feel."

"Look, I'm too…too unnerved to know how I feel."

Buddy sighed. Parker recognized embarrassment.

"Why are you here now? Why are you telling me this when you could have shown up—"

"Years ago," Buddy said.

"Yeah. Years!" Parker grumbled to himself. Impatience flowed from him. "What was the mistake?"

The pause that resulted brought the conversation to suppression and darkness. Buddy was searching the words. Parker enjoyed his father's discomfort.

"Have you done any heroin?" Buddy said.

Parker had studied the musicians and the times from the 1940s on and knew well what had taken place. He had memorized a list of several dozen who had suffered from their addictions or, especially so, those who had died from them. He actually smiled with the recollection that he had asked his mother, when he was twelve, why, instead of naming him Parker, she had not named him John Coltrane Evans. April had laughed. On occasion she sang like Charlie Parker played, which caused Parker such delight that she wrote a tune named "Bird's Havin' Fun." It was named after Charlie and based on a lick of his that she loved, which she dedicated to Parker and sang whenever Parker was in the audience.

Charlie Parker. Parker sighed. "I've stayed away from all that."

"Well, I tried and tried to stay away." Buddy took the lapels of his jacket into his hands and pulled them close to each other. He appeared to want to hide himself within them. "But I failed." He let out a breath. "For years."

"And she left you."

"Yes, even though the horse wasn't enough all on its own."

Parker wondered if maybe it was too late for him to punish Buddy. Parker's actual anger with his father, whoever he may have been, had been palpable. But he now saw that Buddy Briggs was not some soulless monster, as he had figured this disappeared, forgotten man must be. Disappeared, yes. Cast from memory, for sure, although not without continued angry suspicion. But here, in his overcoat, a music teacher, a fedora and muffin, the Harlem School of The Arts, a man seeking forgiveness....

"Although she did hate the heroin," Buddy said.

Parker looked away, into the café. "Of course!"

"Wait, Parker. Please. Let me tell you." Buddy straightened his tie. When he looked up, he saw that Parker's impatience was turning to exasperation. "There's more."

Parker kept still. After a moment, he spoke. "Look, I've had two questions about you, almost since I was born."

Buddy rested a hand on the table, its fingers clenching and loosening.

"Simple questions." Parker was besieged by the irony that, after so many years of sequestering these questions in silence, he actually was now about to liberate them. "'Who was he?' is one of them."

"What's the other?"

"'Where is he?'"

 Buddy removed his overcoat and folded it on the bench to his side. He placed the fedora on top of it. His hair was very close-cut and white. Parker, wondering from where this excessive neatness had come...in the midst of an addiction, in the lies Parker assumed Buddy must have told his mother, in his maybe scattered, certainly sudden abandonment of her....

"She wanted me to go solo," Buddy said. "Maybe you remember she liked all that jazz-funk stuff. You know, the 1970s."

"I do. John McLaughlin. Wayne Shorter."

"Especially Miles, of course."

Parker grinned. All that music was now long gone, but he remembered sitting with his mother as a ten-year-old and listening to some of those records, which even then were marked by age. The rugged rhythms and accents on them, the guitars, the insistence on the probability that you would get up and dance around the world if only to hear more of it. April had once said to her son, shaking her head, "It's not for me, Parker. I couldn't sing to it. But listen to it anyway. Just listen to it!"

Parker still had those records.

"She thought there was a place for me in it…you know, as a front man."

Parker laughed. "Did she want you to wear those hippy clothes, like Miles did?"

Buddy nodded. He too appeared briefly gleeful. Briefly. "She did. She bought the clothes for me. She told me what to wear." He looked down at his tie and the front of the shirt, smoothing them. "It's been a while since I—"

"You don't still have them?"

"I do. But I'd be kind of embarrassed." Buddy adjusted the knot of his tie. "I'm, you know, seventy-three."

"You said there's more, Buddy."

"Yes, we argued."

"About what?"

"I didn't think at the time that any woman should be telling me what to do on my instrument."

Parker took this in with considerable disappointment.

"You know, what kind of music I should play."

His father was one of those complainers. He imagined Buddy sitting on a wooden stool on the stand, listening to April's criticisms while fingering his silly Jimmy Hendrix feathers and red felt pants, the flower-power shirt and the Elton John-style sunglasses, fuming at her. *What the fuck does this bitch know?*

"She had fired me. Often."

"But she took you back?"

"She did. She—"

"That's unheard of!"

"I know. I watched her fire many guys. But, Parker…. She, she—" Buddy looked to the floor.

"She got rid of a ton of musicians."

"That's right." Buddy took in a breath, held it as though considering its worth, and let it out. "The mistake was that I just continued arguing with her. She wouldn't let it go."

"No, no, Buddy."

Buddy held up.

"*You* wouldn't let it go."

Buddy's eyes fell toward the floor once more.

"And that was your mistake."

Buddy swallowed, turned to the side, and looked out onto Grant Avenue. The neighborhood here retains the feel of post-earthquake San Francisco, a century before the recent corporate tsunami of tech companies came ashore. Few buildings on this stretch of Grant Avenue have more than two floors, and almost every one of them has a ground-floor storefront, a bar, or a club. Generally, the music issuing from their doors is decades-old blues, soul, or jazz, not very well played serenades to the much-faded paint on the buildings. The occupants of the clubs often look as decrepit as the storefronts themselves.

Looking up the street himself, Parker recalled the many times he had been sent on an errand to the Liguria Bakery a couple blocks away. April would have given him the Saturday morning task of buying a few slices of its *focaccia*.

"I was good on that horn, Parker."

"I expect you were. April wouldn't have hired you."

"And except for those clothes, I was good at that kind of music. You know, I *played* with Shorter. I *played* with Keith Jarrett." Buddy shrugged. "For a short time."

"On any of their records?"

Buddy appeared stricken, even ill for a moment. "Well…no."

"The heroin?"

"Yes."

"I don't expect she wanted you back either."

Buddy leaned to the side. His right hand fell to the bench as though he had received some sort of blow. "I tried."

"What did she say?"

"And there was the night I hit her."

"You what?"

"I—"

"Nobody hit my mother."

"Twice," Buddy said.

Parker struggled with the quickening, deepened hatred for Buddy that now invaded him. There was much conversation in the café, but Parker heard none of it.

"She wanted me off the heroin, of course. She saw I had lost my…abilities? They'd been overcome, see?"

"By your habit."

"Yes, and I preferred the habit."

"The music didn't matter?"

"Not then." Buddy shrugged. "No."

"And that made her angry."

"Very."

"And she wouldn't shut up."

"Right. So…." Buddy's voice quieted to a simple expelled breath.

Parker's hands lay open, palms down, on his knees, and he could feel what seemed to be their own articulate wish to smother this guy…this monster sitting across from him.

"It was then that she *really* threw me out," Buddy said.

"Good. I don't blame her."

"I haven't either since that day. I haven't had the right to." Buddy took up his fedora and fingered its brim. "She was pregnant." Doing so gave him the appearance of an afflicted elder, addled and searching.

"Did you try to contact her?"

"For years."

"And she turned you down."

"Flat."

"That's good, too."

"Ten years ago was the latest," Buddy said. "In New York."

"I don't believe she would entertain such a thing."

"She knew I loved her, Parker. I stopped the heroin. It was the most ferocious physical difficulty I ever…ever…. I haven't done any of it since before you were born. I apologized so often, and she never told me not to apologize. She always listened to my apologies."

"Although she didn't let you back in."

"Never."

Parker recalled one Saturday morning when he had returned home from the Liguria, the paper-wrapped slices of *focaccia* tied with a string. He was fifteen. He placed the key into the front door lock of their apartment and ran up the entry stairs.

"Mom!"

The apartment door clattered shut behind him, and he threw his jacket onto a chair, took the package into both hands, and hurried toward the living room. He knew April would want to cut two slices from the bread and eat them right away, a custom mother and son cherished together. He stopped after a few steps, though, intimidated by what he heard.

"I don't want to talk with you!"

April's speaking voice had little of the authority with which she sang. Parker had noticed this among a number of the singers to whom she had introduced him. It was as though they had two voices…one for the routine effort of getting through the day; the other for the expression of such magic as their souls contained. In his mother's case, it was a trove of magic like few others. But now, on the phone….

April let out a stifled moan. "Please don't do this!"

Parker held the package tightly in his fingers.

"I know that. I understand it. But you know how I feel."

She was silent.

"Of course, he doesn't know!"

She listened a moment longer, and then hung up the phone. Parker remained quiet in the hallway. *Who was this?* He held the bread close. His heart felt like a stone cut into shards. It hurried, and, doing so, it hurt.

"Parker?"

He took a step toward the living room.

"Parker?"

He found April sitting on the couch. The light coming in the front windows was brightening with the morning. A few sheets of hand-written charts lay next to her. She wore dark red slacks, a red and black silk blouse, and a Mexican tooled leather belt. As it was on stage, April's appearance was gloriously neat, with a stylish nod to Paris, where she now bought most of her clothes. Her black hair, which was full with loose curls and quite long, was gathered behind her head in a tortoise-shell barrette. She was wearing glasses, an addition to her appearance that April usually apologized for. She felt that glasses interfered with her beauty, which for Parker was considerable, despite the fact that he knew he had inherited her short-sightedness. "I like *your* glasses, Parker," she had once said. "I just don't like *mine*." He had laughed with the following line from his mother. "Don't worry, it's nothing personal." He laughed because he knew how personal it indeed was for April herself, who hated her glasses. Her appearance mattered, she reminded him now and then, because it was so featured on her album covers, and she wanted to have her looks on the stand project the same insistence on quietly projected sensuality that the photography emphasized. It was a signature of her singing of ballads. Parker, respectful of April's performance standards, supported how she felt.

But that morning, she had responded to Parker's demand to know who was it on the phone with the news that it was a business thing, her agent… trouble getting paid…. "You know, Parker. The usual."

Now Parker lowered his head. *It wasn't her agent*, he thought. His hands remained on his knees.

"Parker?"

It was Buddy.

He looked up. Buddy's eyes rested on his.

"Forgive me. Please."

Had Buddy broken down in this moment and wept…had sorrow drowned him, Parker would not have responded. That would have been, for him, proof of gross insincerity. Tears were meant to be fresh. Weeping comes from a moment's unpreparedness. But Parker realized that Buddy had been thinking about this for forty years, and so he accepted the re-signed sadness that made Buddy's face so immobile. His eyes were like carved obsidian set in place by proven personal guilt.

But Parker still could not excuse him.

A week later, the concert hall was filling. The loud talk among the audience was filled with congratulatory humor. It felt to Parker, who was to introduce the musicians and say something about his mother, that these people indeed loved her. Everyone in the hall. The talk and noise, the laughter and the sense that great music was about to erupt filled the room.

The musicians came on stage and took their places. Just their arrival caused raucous noise. There would be a couple of marquee singers…Kitty Margolis and Gregory Porter…plus a few other surprise guests.

Parker studied his few notes. When he came onstage to applause, the house lights were still on, and Parker saw Buddy standing, leaning against a side wall at the back. He studied him a moment, until Buddy nodded. Parker smiled and approached the microphone.

"Good evening, everyone."

Applause broke from the crowd, which Parker acknowledged.

"Just a moment, please, if you don't mind." He looked up toward Buddy. "Let's talk more, afterwards."

Buddy nodded. The audience looked around. His black suit shrouded him with grief, as it had at the Caffe Trieste. The overcoat hung from his arm like a much-considered regret. It was clear that no one recognized him.

"A close acquaintance of mine," Parker explained.

SIMONE'S SORROWS

Reynaldo had hoped the novel would give him an opening to forgiveness. In it, a twelve-year-old American girl named Devorah Wiseman goes to France with her parents for a summer vacation in the 1950s. While there, she discovers that her mother, Joanna, had an illegitimate child as a teenager in California. The family were conservative Jews; so, this new addition was a scandal for them, and the baby was given up to a Jewish adoption agency, much to Joanna's deep sorrow. But now, that baby shows up again, by coincidence, now a pretty Parisian in her twenties named Simone Beyle. When Devorah learns of Simone's true identity, she takes it upon herself to introduce her new sister to their mother. The resultant difficulties break apart the marriage of Devorah's parents and reveal the deep emotional troubles that Simone has had throughout her life. Devorah stays on in Paris with her mother Joanna, to navigate the troubles between her sister and their mother…. There is also Simone's American lover, Ray.

And therein lay the novel Reynaldo Nevin subsequently wrote, titled *Simone's Sorrows*.

This was the last book he ever attempted without making a preliminary outline. Reynaldo just started writing the thing, beginning with the title, in a feverish hurry. Because of that, the first draft took him seven years. He finally understood that, without a plan, you can wander and wander up and down the darkness-beset hallways of your manuscript, running into closed doors, turning back, scratching your head, going in some different direction to some other closed door. He suspected this is one of the reasons so many wannabe fiction writers give up so quickly.

Reynaldo did complete that first draft, in 1992. But the writing was so loose-limbed and conflicted, so much a gathering of confused and unrelated themes that, together, they made up a story that was way too long, and very short on plot. He seemed confused about Simone herself. Didn't know quite how to present her. Didn't know what she meant to it all. He let the manuscript sit for three or four months, read the thing again, and put it in a drawer. Literally.

Simone's Sorrows went with Reynaldo through various turns of life and travels during the next twenty-five years. He was married three times and three times divorced. No children. He never looked at the manuscript. Luckily it was also the first manuscript he had ever transcribed to a computer, his new Macintosh LC II. He saved the book on floppy discs. So, it was always nagging at him through subsequent wives and computers… clearing its throat, beckoning to him, muttering disappointment as he wrote and published other books.

What brought him back to it in 2017 was the beloved title and the fact that he so loved Paris. (He had lived there for two years in the late 1960s.) He released the manuscript from its long confinement. The printed-out version was on sheets of paper 8.5 x 11 inches. The paper itself was now mottled brown and yellow. The writing was quite often confusing because the last edit he had made so long ago, which he had not transcribed to floppies, was in pencil. It featured his usual clumsy penmanship, innumerable smeared erasures, lost logic from one point to another, arrows, underlines, and scratch-outs.

Nonetheless, he read it. Yes, it was still confusing. The author did not know what he had here, and so was flying blind. But there was something to it. Simone and her new little sister, Devorah, were so interesting together. Simone's relationship with her unexpected mother was complicated, sometimes badly conflicted, but negotiable…although Simone was so resentful of her mother that the task Devorah was taking on appeared often unresolvable. And, sadly, there was Ray, who Reynaldo now found naïve and unconvincing.

And there *was* Paris.

It is as difficult to write badly as it is to write well. But Paris gives you an advantage right from the beginning because it so lends itself to inspired description. Reynaldo subscribed to the notion that you should write about the surroundings in a particular scene in such a way that the surroundings themselves comment on the emotions of the characters. A teacup can be described countlessly, one way after another. So why not describe it so that it helps reveal the feelings of the characters themselves? A teacup so described can help the reader understand better what's happening in the mind of the person holding it, or in that of the person watching how it is being held. Etc.

So, Reynaldo had made a point of describing Simone's reactions to the city of Paris differently, depending on what she was learning about herself, her mother, her sister, and Ray.

Reynaldo started examining the novel again. The process was no easier than before. The mistakes and failings that had existed in 1992 still had to be dealt with. *But basically*, he thought, *it isn't bad!* He cut and cut, wrote and re-wrote, suffered the renewals of self-doubt, anger, and exhaustion, cut some more, savaged the thing, put it back together....

And now *Simone's Sorrows* was out! Although Reynaldo thought it would be better to say that, now, Simone's sorrows *were* out.

Simone. He had missed her since the day she left him in 1970.

That day, they were sitting in the Place des Vosges, and Simone was weeping. She did not understand how Reynaldo could have done what he did. His response, that "all men do it, Simone," had caused a caustic tear-laden outburst from her. His French by this time was good enough for him to understand fully the surly profanities she used.

Reynaldo knew his excuse was at best some sort of ploy to make him seem, to himself, French-sophisticated. If all men had affairs, he was simply doing what comes naturally. This was self-delusion, though, and he knew it. Such blithe French sophistication is, indeed, clear French foolishness. Acknowledging what he had done, accepting his responsibility for it, and asking Simone's forgiveness might have gotten the same response from her. But at least Reynaldo would not be offering a made-up flippancy, which his "all men" remark had been.

—

He had finished going over his first published copy of *Simone's Sorrows* and was reading it again now while seated on one of the benches in South Park. Reynaldo came here from his office around the corner on Second

Street every fair-weather weekday, enjoying the fact that he was so much a San Francisco local. His great-great-great-grandfather Reynaldo Chacón, a Californio whose business dealings had somehow escaped the clutches of the arriviste *gringuitos* who had won the War of 1846, had continued a life of land purchases (two *ranchos* near Spanishtown, on the coast south of San Francisco, and several large plots far out on what was to become Third Street in the city itself) and personal investments. To help out struggling Mark Hopkins, Reynaldo Chacón had made a $500.00 investment in 1861 in the Central Pacific Railroad, the returns on which, multiplied by other savvy deals, made him a multi-millionaire. His sons and grandchildren had sued each other for years after his death. The final, reduced fortune, having enriched several law firms and the grandchildren who had been victorious in the lawsuits, had eventually settled upon the novelist Reynaldo Nevin… so named "Reynaldo" at his mother's request, despite his father's being an Irish immigrant furniture maker on Potrero Hill. Reynaldo had been freed of the obligation to work for a living, and he had the good fortune of being talented with words. Even as a child, he told a good story. So now, at the age of seventy-six, he was going through this, his seventh published novel. He was happy with it, as, with a few caveats, were *The New York Times* and others. They felt that Reynaldo's treatment in the novel of the American character Ray was thin…a little pallid…certainly not up to the complex nuances of Simone's remarkable, conflicted personality.

But in the end, a little miffed, Reynaldo thought he had done better with Ray than *The New York Times* thought.

Reynaldo Nevin was an elegant man. Especially on this day, which was of silvery Spring sunshine and slight breezes flowing over the park from the bay a few blocks away, he was dressed with bohemian grace. First there was the beret, classic dark blue, bought fifty years ago in Paris and worn at a tilt. A flowered silk kerchief was tied around his neck, the V-shaped lower end of it held secure by the collar of his black dress shirt. He also wore tailored black wool slacks, and his slim black leather jacket took fifteen years off his age. This was his nod to the beatniks whom his father had excoriated in the 1950s for their profligate ways and, especially, their indecipherable sentences (or, as Reynaldo's father called it, "whatever it is they think they're up to with that drivel.") As a little boy in San Francisco, Reynaldo had liked the beatniks. Especially the berets. He thought they were funny-looking and, so, worth the appreciative laughter they caused in him. As a student at Berkeley he had finally read their stuff and found some of it pretty good. Some of it. He still liked their dress better than their verse and emulated it.

When he had arrived in Paris in 1968, during the aftermath of the revolt that year, he found that the Beat look was still the rage. He fit right in, although at the time he had little French. That changed, with time and with Simone, who taught him so well, aided by their intimacy, that when she got rid of him, he was fluent.

He put the book down on his lap. As on every day since she walked away so upset with him, he thought of Simone now. She too had been a bohemian of a sort. From Aix-en-Provence, she spoke with an Occitan accent so different from the Parisian that she was noted by her friends for it. She had told Reynaldo that her mother had wished her to lose the accent and had sent her to a locution teacher from Paris who was married to an Occitan. Simone could speak "proper French" when her mother asked her to. But she enjoyed the southern bite of the Aix accent, especially now that she was living in Paris. She used it to distinguish herself from the other musicians trying to make it there.

Simone had not studied music formally. Picking up her piano chops from records and in Aix cafes, she had come into her own as an accompanist in small Paris jazz clubs. Reynaldo was writing by then. His first novel and then his second were both unpublishable.

"Mr. Nevin?"

Reynaldo looked up. A lovely young woman. He had noticed her a moment before, sitting on a bench across South Park. She had been watching him. Now much closer to him than when he had first seen her, she did indeed take his breath. In her late twenties—

"I have a copy of your book." She reached into her shoulder bag and brought it out. Like Reynaldo's own copy, it appeared barely breached. The dust jacket had no wrinkles or abrasions. The card from Green Apple Books stuck out from inside like a tiny flag. She looked at Reynaldo's photo on the back cover, which showed him standing next to the statue of Cervantes in Golden Gate Park. He realized the relationship of his work to that of Cervantes was, well, distant. But so be it. The statue was there…so why not? At the photographer's suggestion, he had glanced at the camera, and the recollection of the vanity that had taken him over for that moment came to him once again. He didn't usually pay attention to such things. But he did like this picture. It reminded him of another that Simone had taken of him in Paris.

"Will you sign it?" The woman took a pen from her bag, holding it up between the index finger and thumb of her right hand. The look on her face was familiar to him. It conveyed the sweet, humorous expectation that an authorial refusal from him might be coming. She spoke with an accent. French…but from where? He would not refuse, but even if he did, it would be kindly because of her accent.

"Of course." Reynaldo took the book from her, opened it to the title page, and she handed him the pen. "Your—"

"My name?"

"Yes."

She gave him a smile, cocking her head to the side to watch his hand-writing. "Her name is my name."

"Simone?"

She tightened her lips, so that a possible frown appeared. "Yes," she said. "Simone de Carcassona."

Reynaldo autographed the book and handed it back to her.

"It's such a nice day," he said. "Would you join me for coffee?"

Simone nodded. She was enthused, he surmised, by the prospect of a conversation with the author. She had in her appearance and her dress a kind of Parisian attention to stylish, well-honed finesse. Her dress was very lightly lemon-colored, simple, and complimented by the silk scarf she was wearing about her shoulders, from which flared all manner of images of flowers: fuschias, peonies, and marigolds. She was glorious with them. Her hair, dark brown, curled, and full down to her shoulders, contrasted with the dress and with the very red lipstick she was wearing. Reynaldo reflected a moment on what a pleasant conversation this was going to be for him, and he excused himself, to get the coffee. When he returned to the bench from the café at one edge of the park, Simone was reading in the book. She closed it as he sat down and took the coffee from him.

"Where are you from," he said.

"Paris."

Reynaldo did not reply. He was stirring sugar into his own coffee and, as the slim wooden stick swirled about in the tall paper cup, he suspected that, somehow, he may know her.

"You heard of this book there?" he said.

"Yes."

"How so?"

"I'm a translator, English to French, for the Paris government."

"The Hôtel de Ville?"

"Yes, that's where I work. So, I read a lot of American newspapers. That's where I learned about your new novel."

"Thank you. It's nice to have—"

"But that's not why I'm here."

"The novel, you mean."

"The book is peripheral," Simone said. "But it gave me a reason to search you out."

Reynaldo swallowed.

"I told her I would," Simone said.

"Who?"

"My grandmother." Simone looked to the left, shielding a passage of sorrow. "Simon Beyle. You know…. She loved you"

"Simone, I—"

"She did." Simone looked out across the park. A breeze riffled the trees above. It was a thought, little more, in the weather's passage. She pushed back a lock of hair behind her right ear, and Reynaldo recognized the gesture. Even the way she held her fingers was a mannerism he knew. "And you've got that here in this book," she said.

"I do?"

"I recognize her, Mr. Nevin."

Reynaldo's lips tightened. "Please, Simone." He glanced at the book on his lap, which he had shut. "It's Reynaldo. Please."

Simone remained silent.

"How is she?"

More silence intervened. "She's gone." Her eyes turned down. "She was happy. She loved her children…my father and my aunt Antonia. All of us." Simone let out a breath. "She and I especially traveled a lot together. She brought me to the U.S. my first time when I was in secondary school."

"Where?"

"Cours Moliére, in the twelfth."

"No, I mean here, in the United States."

"Oh." Simone grinned. "New York." She looked away. "San Francisco."

Reynaldo leaned to the side, grasping his hands. He inclined his head, examining the hands where they lay on the cover of his book. "I'm sorry she didn't call me."

"Reynaldo. Please. She wouldn't…. After what—"

Reynaldo began shaking his head, lowering his eyes.

"She always knew you were here." A second breeze passed across Simone, and she let her hair settle where it would. "She had told me about you in Paris. Many times. And where you lived in this country."

Reynaldo looked up.

"My grandmother and I were very close. She couldn't call you. She wouldn't."

"Because of—"

"Yes."

"Because of what happened?"

"No." Simone seemed lost in unsought silence. She searched about for what to say. "Because of what you did."

She removed a leather folder from her bag and brought out a photograph. The folder itself was old, partially ruined, its leather overtaken by many years of lying about in some drawer or other, Reynaldo guessed. It was black, but where the leather had cracked, it was aged brown and yellow. A pair of gold-leafed initials had been stamped into its front cover, the letters "SB" and "RN." "My sister and I found it after she died. It had all sorts of things in it. Love letters…yours. And there was a camera, which was one of those American Kodaks, the…the….” Simone frowned.

“The Brownie,” Reynaldo said.

“That's it, yes. She called it 'My 127.'”

“It was the model number.”

“You had one?”

“No, but….” Reynaldo took in a breath. “I remember Simone's.”

Simone handed the photo to Reynaldo. It showed him sitting on a bench in the Place des Vosges. A black-and-white, it too was creased with age. The margin around the photo was more the color of brown-stained honey, its original only here and there white. The lower right corner was sheared off at the fingers of the young man who was the subject of the photo. Reynaldo had still had his beard then and was amused now by how carefully trimmed and combed it appeared. Its rakish authority was com-plimented by the beret he was wearing in the photo. It was the same one he had on now. The background of the photo showed a few of the trees that are always in the square. The buildings, though, were different from what is there now. The Place des Vosges in 1970 was close to ruin. The buildings had received so little care in the twentieth century that their clear elegance was just as clearly diminished. A playground for the aristocracy when it was first christened in 1612, Place des Vosges seemed in 1970 a luxurious, poorly maintained slum.

The picture had charmed Reynaldo.

———

He and Simone had come to the Place des Vosges often to sit beneath the trees. “You think you can resolve your duplicity by saying that all men do it?” Simone had said that particular day. She glanced at the three daffodils Reynaldo had brought with him, gathered with some frivolous greens, what he hoped would smooth the waters that had stirred so violently the day be-fore. A slip of the tongue had revealed what he had been doing. Simon was to be on the bandstand this particular night at a small club in Montmartre. It was special, since she was for the first time the leader of the group. No singer. Just drums, a bass, and a sax, all backing up Simone Beyle. She had a flare for intricate improvisation that reminded friends of McCoy Tyner, although she had a softer touch, not nearly so driven by testosterone as was McCoy's. Simone's music was very adventurous, but never thundered, never went through the roof. Reynaldo himself thought he discerned something of Debussy in her playing. Simone's improvisations floated. On occasion, they took your breath with their so sought-after wanderings. For him, she was clearly French in her playing, even clearly Parisian.

"Simone, I—

"And here in this beautiful place, on this day, the day of my first solo, you persist in this idea that all men do it…" She turned away. "What do you Americans call it? my first solo…first—"

"Gig," Reynaldo said.

"Yes. How can you do this, on this day? To me?"

"Simone, please, I—"

"You've told me so often how much you love me, and now, now…. This!"

"We're free, both you and I," he said. He sat back on the bench and folded his arms before him. "You—"

"I am not free. I'm a Jew."

"I know that."

"We do not betray each other."

"Well—"

"At least the Jews I know don't. Would you like *me* to betray *you*?"

"Of course not, Simone. I didn't—"

"You didn't betray me?"

"No. I had an affair. That's not betrayal."

"What is it, then? Just…what's the French phrase? *"En rut"*?

Reynaldo shrugged. "Simone."

"What's the English?"

"The same. 'Rutting.'"

Simone stood up from the bench. Her bag dropped to the ground. A black leather folder fell from it. It was new, and had two sets of gold-leaf initials, side by side, on the lower front cover. Simone had told him the day she bought it that it was for reminiscences. It was for love. She would keep photos in it, notes, letters, recollections of some affectionate event or exchange between the two of them, more photos. Swearing, she picked it up now, tossed it back into her bag, and took a few steps away from Reynaldo.

"I'm leaving."

"Simone—"

"Leave me alone!"

"You don't have to do this."

"*Trou du cul!*" Simone walked away. She gripped the bag to her chest. When she turned her head, a small spray of tears hurried to the ground. Her lips were pressed to each other, although she had no difficulty with the next utterance: "*Fils de pute!*"

—

Simone, taking up the coffee Reynaldo had brought to her, fingered the leather folder. "You used her so badly, Reynaldo."

"But do you think I use her badly here?" Reynaldo pointed to the cover of his book.

"No. The way you describe Simone...." Simone nodded. "She's my grandmother. In the book, she's in her twenties, I know. But she's *ma grand-mère.*" Simone perused the folder for a moment. She sighed. "*Oh, mémère. Je t'aime.*"

"Simone, I—"

"You describe her perfectly."

Reynaldo had attempted when he first was writing the book to simply describe the relationship between the young American and his French Jewish girlfriend. It was secondary to the main plot. But Reynaldo had felt that real care was necessary. More than anything else, in the character of Ray, he had himself in mind. Yes, Simone Beyle was the principal figure. But for Ray's character, this would be a coming-of-age piece. Ray's introduction to love. Ray's own Simone.... Reynaldo was respectful of the importance of creating all characters whole. So, he would not let this Ray fellow be just "the boyfriend." In the final writing, he worked on Ray more than on anyone else.

"Perfectly?" Reynaldo sipped from his own coffee. "How so?" he asked.

"The way Simone's reactions to Ray tell you so much about him." Simone opened the book. "And about her, of course." She thumbed through several pages. "Ray doesn't know himself at all, you know, and it's ingenious how you've made Simone be the character who actually understands what kind of man he is. What kind of confused...." She pointed at the cover. "He's clueless, this American, and you learn as much as you would ever want to know about him because of how Simone feels. She's the true character in the book, the one who has such genuine heart, and you describe that so well." Simone shook her head. "She has her family history, and the American has nowhere near the soul and vision that Simone has. And that's what you caught in her. You write so...what is it? so 'tellingly?' of her." Simone lowered her eyes. Her chin wavered. "This is my grandmother here. I see her in every sentence you wrote about her."

"You know, she told me I was a fool," Reynaldo said.

"Yes, she told me about that, too." Simone reached out a hand, and Reynaldo passed the picture back to her. Her eyes were wistful, a moment's pleased recollection. "When my sister found this folder.... She was examining it as though here was some sort of unknowable sensation from a century ago. There were other photos in the folder, many of the two of you. But this photo was on top. There were pictures of my grandmother, too. As a five-year-old. In Hebrew school. Her parents." Simone nodded, her head aslant as a further thought passed through her. "Herself at the piano."

Reynaldo remembered that photo. He had taken it. Simone leaning against the piano in the club on Montmartre, a few days before her gig. She was so excited that day that she could barely hold herself still for the picture. The piano was slightly out of tune, and she had just had an argument, in Reynaldo's presence, with the club owner about it. An Algerian, he had laughed at her criticisms of the piano. "You should be happy I gave you this chance, Simone. We don't headline women here. You should feel privileged." He had taken up the wrinkled, torn-open packet of Gauloise cigarettes from the bar table at which they were sitting. "And a Jew, too!" He wore a white shirt, its buttons opened to the middle of his chest. "I don't know how you Jews do it!" He sensed he was very handsome. Perhaps he had been so at one time. But now he appeared simply harried, well on his way to grey hair, sagging cheeks, and resentful indolence. He turned to Reynaldo as he put the packet into a shirt pocket and offered a gentlemanly smile. "You know, women don't play well."

Reynaldo remained silent. He glanced toward Simone, whose eyes were so fixed on the Algerian's smile that Reynaldo knew she hated him. She would get through this gig, get her money, get the hoped-for celebratory reviews, and immediately abandon this idiot's Montmartre dump. There were plenty of other dumps up here.

As they descended the hill toward the river, Reynaldo wished to soften Simone's unhappiness.

"You shouldn't worry so much about that."

"About what?"

"What he said about the Jews."

Simone moved a few steps away from him. When he turned to look, he saw that her mouth had tightened and that she was gripping her handbag close.

"I mean, those times are gone, aren't they?"

Reynaldo called Simone a few days after the gig, which she had told him not to attend. He hoped a congratulation from him would soften Simone's hurt feelings. A critic from the French *Jazz Magazine* had been in the audience. Explaining that he had gone to the club in order to see the work between the drummer and the bassist, who were already reasonably well-known, he went on at some length to congratulate this young pianist who, he wrote in his last few sentences, "despite her gender, plays well indeed. I'll tell you the truth. I didn't expect it. To my ultimate pleasure, I found that she is quite beyond amateur."

Simone did not pick up the phone. Nor did she call Reynaldo. He wrote to her, an apology. She did not write back.

—

"She loved the piano, and she even got a little famous…for a few years." Simone replaced the folder in her bag. "You know, it does surprise me that your Ray in here…" She fingered the book. "…doesn't figure much in it."

"I'm sorry?"

"It's clear that you think he's an important character. But this Simone… she's…she's—"

"The one that matters?"

"Of course, Reynaldo." Simone laughed, a quiet glee. "Do you think you paid so much more attention to her here because you wished to avoid yourself?"

Reynaldo remained silent.

Simone pointed to the cover of the book. "Did you wish to forgive yourself with this?"

Again, he could not summon an answer.

"Because, you know, it's too late for my grandmother to forgive you." She sipped from her coffee and placed the cup on the bench next to her. "She wished to. She always wished to."

"Then why do you think she didn't?"

Simone let out a breath, studying the cover for a long moment.

"I think it is that…she didn't think you cared at all about love."

Reynaldo's face tightened. He could feel it leathering.

"She told me so, many times," Simone said. "You thought you didn't need to be forgiven. You wouldn't value her forgiveness, she said. You would betray her even more because of it…she said."

Reynaldo's missing Simone for so many years now suddenly felt fraudulent to him, although he knew it wasn't. He was sure he *had* loved her. But her granddaughter's study of his face just in this moment was filled with saddened, accusatory stricture.

"And you clearly don't get the Jews." Simone replaced the folder and book in her bag and stood up. "Thanks for the coffee, Ray."

She walked from the bench. It seemed to Reynaldo that his novel now, hidden away as it was in her bag and silent, had sprung to freedom. But… freedom from him! What lived in it was Simone Beyle, and little else drew attention. Simone Beyle herself was left, her sorrows so clarified, her resentment so genuine, her love ruined. Reynaldo realized what was happening. Simone had lived a happy life. She had had her children. She had her own Simone, the granddaughter traveling the world with her. If Reynaldo had really loved Simone when they were young in Paris, this granddaughter Simone never would have come to be. Reynaldo did not wish that upon her, although she had just revealed to him, in the way her grandmother once had attempted to do, his shallow pointlessness.

STOW LAKE

Joe Bright's thoughts returned to Billie Holiday, as they usually did when he was waiting for his father. A retired trauma surgeon, Samuel Bright was an enormous fan of Lady Day's singing, especially the recordings— "Such soulful longing", Samuel often said while listening to them—that she had made with the pianist Oscar Peterson. Now, so many years removed from Joe's time as a Navy corpsman with the Marines, he recalled the day that he and his father had talked about Billie, just before Joe had left San Francisco for Vietnam. He had been nineteen, a big fan of Marvin Gaye and Jimi Hendrix, about whose amazing talents he had never been able to convince his father.

Hendrix was a lot of noise for Samuel Bright. "A pretty boy in all that orange and red get-up, all those feathers and make-up". He also couldn't play the guitar, as far as Samuel was concerned. Marvin Gaye was clearly a gifted singer, but his attitude toward his audience, the over-confidence, the sex, the in-your-face brazen demand to accept everything that Gaye was shoving at you…that made Samuel think that Gaye was more exhibitionist than artist. Samuel believed that popular music itself had been derailed by guys like these, by Miles Davis too and even The Beatles. "Too many gimmicks," he had complained. "No soul. Too much bother about sales. Too much formula."

Billie Holiday, on the other hand, merely had to make a gesture with one of her beautiful be-ringed hands, to look to the side the way she did so often, as though no one else were in the room and she had caught herself in mid-thought, in a passing dream, or a painful effort at a smile…and then all she had to do was sing the words. "*Gay roué and gay divorcée/who lunch at The Ritz,/will tell you that it's…/divine!*" She sang from regret. A ruse, The Divine yet filled The Ritz, a palace devoted to fun and loss. Billie Holiday was the muse who made you feel that fun in your own ruptured heart.

"She recorded it in 1952, with Oscar," Samuel had told his son. "Her voice was failing. It wanders off key sometimes, weakens here and there. But you can tell how much the song is giving her. You know, she sings '*It's good to live it again*' there in the end. She means it, even though she's faltering so badly."

That day in 1967, on a bench overlooking Stow Lake in Golden Gate Park, Samuel had given Joe two eight-track tapes filled with Billie Holiday's music. Dressed as always in a dark three-piece suit, a white dress shirt and dark tie, his hair just beginning to gray that year, his eyeglasses serving to make his face appear opaque and ordered, Samuel took his son's right hand into both of his. "Listen to this while you're over there, Joey. Please. Think about San Francisco. Think about your mother and me. Just listen to this stuff now and then."

Months before, Samuel had pleaded with Joe not to go into the Navy. "Finish college. Go to medical school. The world doesn't need another piece of cannon fodder. It does need another doctor."

But Joe had gone to Vietnam and been wounded at Khe Sanh in 1968.

There had been no medical school after he had recovered, a painful realization for his father, who could not understand why such a talented kid as Joey would want to waste his time with words. "What do you think, you're a Hemingway?"

Joe often thought about that moment, too, when he and his father had been seated on this very same bench two years later. Stow Lake appeared motionless in the uncustomary hot San Francisco weather, one of the three or four days a year in that city in which the heat holds to your skin as though bandaged to it. Indeed, Joe's legs were heavily bandaged that day, his recovery from the burns progressing reasonably enough, although, as Samuel told him, "that skin below your knees, it's so bad that it'll always be like cowhide, Joey. But cowhide that breaks open if you bang it against a low table or something. It'll itch. It'll hurt"

And so it had, and so it did now as he listened to more of Billie Holiday on his iPhone.

Holding the eight-tracks in his hands before Joe left for Vietnam, his father had described to him the one Billie Holiday concert he had attended, on March 27, 1948 at Carnegie Hall in New York. Samuel was twenty-seven that year, doing his surgery residency at the Mount Sinai hospital. He had no time for anything, with a new baby about to arrive…Joey himself. But Samuel made time for this concert.

"Your mother and I were up in the first balcony. First row. And there were so many people…black people, white people… Not an empty seat in the place. Looking down on the main floor, I don't know if I've ever seen such…splendor in an audience. Gorgeous women, black and white, dressed beautifully. Tuxes. Money. The love they had for her."

Samuel looked to his hands.

"You never heard a voice like that, Joey. She did more than thirty tunes that night, and every one of them—every one—took your breath."

Three months after his deployment, lying against a red mud embankment on Hill 881, smoke rising from his legs, his helmet rolling down the slime and mud beside him, everything about Joe was mottled red and black with mud except where his right shoulder bled. A bright carmine gleaming. The piece of shrapnel that had loosed the helmet from his head had been diverted into the shoulder itself. Joe fell into a pain-ridden swoon, in which, through all the noise of the explosions and sear and automatic rifle fire, broken slivers of music ran through his mind, just here and there, gone in the terrifying pain, a sigh of remorse, death demanding that it be heard. Oscar Peterson's recollected piano so sweet in the roar. Billie Holiday singing for Joe despite the fact that his legs were on fire and he was dying.

"Come on, Joey." Someone huddled down next to him, still under fire, his voice barely controlled, all anger and panic. "We're gettin' you out." Joe didn't know who it was, even though he recognized the voice. They dragged him by his shoulders out of the kill zone. He figured he was dead. Black smoke rose from the tattered shreds of his pants legs. His own skin… he didn't know what was happening with his own skin.

Joe glimpsed his father approaching, a ninety-year-old now, but still one who enjoyed his exercise. He loved this particular path around Stow Lake, the undulant turns in it, and the trees seeming to bow down over the surface of the lake itself. This bench… Joe mused that it had to be a bench very like this one that Billie had sung about. *"Lovers that bless the dark/On benches in Central Park/Greet autumn in New York."*

He could not remember now whether that too went through his mind as, screaming, held down by others, still under fire, he awaited the med-evac. He should have died.

"*It's good to live it again,*" she sang.

Joe stood up, a cane in each hand. Walking still caused him considerable difficulty, and his father occasionally kidded him for that. "Well, you're sixty-three years old, Joey. What do you expect?" Samuel was a widower with an apartment in The Marina, overlooking the garden and pond of the Palace of Fine Arts. He walked far more comfortably than his son did, and still dressed with natty, businesslike style. A suit and a necktie, always. Dr. Samuel Bright, Professor Emeritus of Surgery, Stanford University Medical Center.

Joe suspected that someone being told about such an exchange would accuse Samuel of heartlessness toward his son. But that was not so. As soon as Joe had arrived at the Brooke Army Burn Center in Texas, Samuel flew there. The physicians explained that Joe had suffered full thickness burns in his lower legs, and that there had not been the facilities in the field to flay the skin, to enable blood circulation. The musculature had quickly deteriorated.

"You've got to do that within a few hours, Doctor Bright," one of the physicians told him. Joe was lying in a bed, his father seated next to it. Samuel placed a hand on Joe's chest, to comfort him, as the doctor continued. "And out there, Joe, where you were…I don't have to tell you about that fire fight you were in. A bad one. Very bad. They just couldn't get you out in time."

Joe had awakened every morning in the burn center to light coming in his window. But it was hardly an awakening. His sleep was not actually sleep. Rather, it was a kind of floating wonder steeped in flame. He could not move, his legs being wrapped in whatever they wrapped them in, and stabilized. "They'll heal," his father told him. "But you're not going to have anything like the mobility you did have. And you'll have pain."

His father took as much time as he could away from his practice, to be with Joe. Joe had always marveled at how Samuel described some of the cases he had in his surgery practice. He could describe the most gruesome details of a patient's situation as though he were arranging milk and orange juice in a refrigerator. Joe had often thought that his father had no emotions when it came to his work. A shoulder splattered by a close-range shotgun blast was simply a disorganized object that Samuel was attempting to put together again, despite the fact that if he didn't, the patient could well die. His descriptions for Joe never included anything about his feelings for having to view so much torn apart carnage.

But at the burn center, listening to Samuel's advice about Joe's own misfortune, Joe sensed the underpinning, unexpected as it may sound, of anguished distress. He had always loved his father, despite Samuel's seeming distance, not knowing quite why he cared for him so. He realized now that his father's feelings had indeed *not* been hidden from him. A run-of-the-mill patient chewed up by a severe knifing would not feel them because Doctor Bright had built the barrier into his demeanor. He needed to save this person's life, and the distance allowed the surgeon to do things right. But for Joe, at the burn center, his father had actually shown clear, invasive pain as he had watched his own son suffer the results of death's not having taken him.

And here at Stow Lake, now, Joe saw once again what his father had successfully hidden from others. From that first moment in Texas, Samuel's commiserative pain was real and demonstrable to Joe, and Joe realized that that was because he and his father shared not just some DNA connection, but a mixing of souls as well. The passage of their pain back and forth was a silent acknowledgment of it for both men. Samuel's emotions were palpable and deep, like Joe's wounds.

These many years later, Samuel still helped Joe wash and hydrate the skin on his legs when he came to visit. They went for weekly walks around Stow Lake. Samuel kept up on the latest for the long-term treatment of such severe wounds. He admired his son's writing and the fact that his novels had done so much to explain the heartfulness of the wounded in war. Joe's first novel had described the death of a Hill 881 corpsman, his thoughts falling to dreams as he lay next to two dead men, both of whom he had thought he could save. Mendoza and Sink had been the two characters' names in the book, the same as the two Marines that Joe was lying next to when they all were hit by the incendiary. Joe's fourth novel, about the last moment in the life, in Vietnam in 1954, of the combat photographer Robert Capa, had made him minorly famous for a while. Throughout the novel, before he stepped on the landmine, Capa's damaging, electrified second thoughts about his life revealed themselves. In the novel, his death did little to relieve his suffering.

The book's fame diminished, and Joe wrote another one, also famous, and then another.

"Hello, Dad." Joe took Samuel's hand in his. Samuel was wearing a Mayser Piero panama that he had owned for years. It was brushed, blocked, in beautiful shape.

"Hello, Joey. How you feeling?" His father looked down at the canes.

"The same. Fine."

"Pain?"

"Sure. But, so what?"

They turned up the path toward the coffee stand at the boat rental shack on the lake, where they stopped for Joe to rest. Arriving at the coffee stand, Samuel told his son that he was buying, and while they stood in line waiting, he turned to Joe to continue the conversation they had been having.

"That's the reason I call it 'Johnson's Folly.'" Samuel took a billfold from his jacket pocket and brought out a twenty. "You know, president on the day you were wounded. But you could call it Kennedy's. Eisenhower's. It doesn't matter." He returned the billfold to its pocket. "I think in my heart that those wounds—yours and those of all the other guys—are insulting reminders to the wounded themselves of how little they mattered."

He took the two cups of coffee into his hands, and both men turned toward an empty metal table with chairs and a view of the lake. Samuel placed the coffees on the table, along with two paper napkins and two plastic-wrapped slices of banana bread. Their usual. He put his hand on the small of Joe's back, caressing it as he took the canes from his son and then helped him sit down.

"They were doing the best they could, Dad."

"Maybe. They did abandon that hill a month or two after you took it." Samuel eased down into his own chair and sipped from his coffee. "Without a word why."

Joe unwrapped one of the pieces of banana bread, tore it into two pieces, and offered one to his father. His books had allowed the rages that overwhelmed him, and his hatred for what had happened on 881, to be channeled into much-savored creativity and a sort of battered peace. He was grateful to have discovered what the writing could do to calm him. He felt that, in many ways, he was still alive because of it.

"Yeah," he said. "I know they did."

—

A soft wind floated from the west…from the ocean…and hurried across Stow Lake. The surface wavered. The water darkened, cold blue to a version of black where the air stirred it. Joe opened the top button of his shirt, to allow the breeze and, as he turned to look across the lake, he saw a young woman and an older man walking along the path toward the boathouse. Both Asians, they seemed as different from each other as one could imagine. The woman was in her early thirties, Joe guessed, very slim and small, dressed in black slacks and a short black cotton jacket. She was wearing sunglasses and just now securing a handbag to her right shoulder. She appeared fresh, pleased, and physically delicate. Looking toward the boat house, she pointed the building out to her companion.

The man was dressed in a suit and tie. He was taller than the woman, although not much. The formality of his clothing made him seem professorial, a quiet assurance that was enhanced by the fact of his walking with a cane. He moved slowly and looked ahead at the pathway as though it were an uphill passage, even though the pathway itself bordered the lake and was therefore flat. His walking was labored. Even this slow stroll was an effort. He was beset with elderly-seeming worry. When his companion pointed out the boat house, he nodded, acknowledging her speaking to him. But clearly, he had to concentrate on his balance.

"Ah, here's someone I've wanted you to meet," Samuel said. "A student of a friend of mine."

"A physician?"

"Yes. Now she is. Emergency room surgery. The same as me, and a real pro." Samuel stood and touched Joe's right shoulder. "Shirley Phạm's her name." He stepped toward the path to greet the couple. "And her grandfather." Samuel waved. "Phạm Cuong"

Joe stood up as the couple approached their table. He leaned on his canes.

There was a quarter hour's small talk. Shirley's medical training in New York City. Her residency at Stanford. Cuong had been a translator at the United Nations: Vietnamese, French, and English. His wife had died a few years ago, and he still lived in New York City. He was visiting his granddaughter just now, with whom it was quite evident he was close.

But Joe sensed that Shirley and Samuel wished to leave the two men alone for a time. "I know you don't know it, Joe," Shirley said. "But you have things to talk about." She stood and kissed her grandfather on the cheek. *"Ông nội."*

"I love you, Shirley," Cuong whispered. He took her right hand a moment with his left, and let it go. "Thank you." His own right hand was a black prosthesis, in the shape of a hand, coming from the sleeve of his suit coat where it rested on the table. So smoothly manufactured, it looked like sculpture, only a sculpture without heart, fashioned for utility alone, and emotionally remote. It did not move.

Samuel and Shirley left the boathouse and, before they set out on the walkway around the lake, he pointed out the rental boats to her. Joe noticed how Shirley glanced over her shoulder as she listened to Samuel's talk. There was worry in the glance.

"Shirley asked me to tell you that I was born in 1945." Cuong sat back and grinned. It was the first instance of liveliness Joe had seen from him. "The Japanese left, and I arrived." He sighed and ran a hand through his thinning grey hair. "Some months before the French came back to Vietnam. My father had worked for the French colonial government before the Second War. He had lived in France…studied there. We spoke as much French at home as we spoke Vietnamese."

"French," Joe said.

"Fluently."

"And he went back to work for them."

"Yes."

"What about your English?"

Cuong fingered the buttons of his jacket with his left hand, studying them. He did not respond immediately, as though he were searching the words…maybe the story itself. "After the American war, in 1980, I was able to go to England. They wanted me to keep an eye on what was happening in Europe." He sipped from his tea. "How the Europeans felt about us." The silence wavered. "The English…. Very good teachers."

"How long were you there?"

"Five years."

"And the American war? Yourself, I mean."

Cuong swallowed. After a long silence, he swallowed once more. "Yes. I fought in the war, also."

Joe glanced at the prosthesis.

"The same as you. Shirley told me about you. Your father had described for her your time there."

"ARVN?" Joe's reference was to the army of South Vietnam.

Cuong looked to the side. "No, I…I…." He sipped from his tea. "I was with the Viet Cong."

Joe swallowed. He waited, not able in the moment to respond.

"Khe Sanh," Cuong said. He leaned forward and gathered his hands on the table. He studied the cup of tea. "Your Hill 881." He looked up. "Your father had told Shirley about your…your experience there."

"Where I…" Joe spread his hands wide and looked down at his legs.

"Yes. And then she told your father about me." Cuong held his right arm out on the table. "That's where I lost this."

Joe examined the prosthesis. Cuong nodded and touched his cane. "And my right leg."

"What happened?"

"Part of the leg. I was running. Crazy. They told me later I was shouting out for my hand. 'Where's my hand?' And one of your M-16s…. It…." He gestured toward his leg.

Joe assented. "I understand."

"They were incredible, those M-16s." Cuong tightened his lips. "Better than our Type-56 rifles. Chinese. Not as good as American."

"And the others with you? They survived?'"

"We were all running."

"They survived?"

"No."

Joe's lips tightened. "Eventually they….?"

Cuong shook his head. "No. Not 'eventually.'" He looked out onto the lake. "Apparently…more or less…instantaneously."

"You don't remember."

"No. They told me after they got me out of there."

"How did they get you out?"

"One of our people carried me. On her back."

Joe waited for more. But for the moment, there was not more. Both men sat quietly. Neither was ill-at-ease. Neither was beset by nerves. For Joe, silence was simply the most respectful manner of expression, given the moment.

"I've read your book about Robert Capa," Cuong said.

Surprise jolted Joe's quiet.

"The French, of course, did not understand the situation," Cuong said. "They thought we would welcome them back, after the Japanese." He smiled. "And when we did not, they punished us."

"But you punished the French, eventually."

"Yes, despite the help they got from your Mr. Eisenhower."

Joe let out a breath. "He didn't understand the situation, either."

Cuong now nodded. He caressed the head of his cane.

Joe continued. "I suppose he felt that, because he had saved France itself—"

Cuong exhaled, a moment of almost silent laughter. "They were as ineffectual at Normandy as they were at Dien Bien Phu," he said.

"What about the French Resistance, though?"

Cuong swallowed, looking to the side. "Yes. The Resistance. They did to the Nazis what we did to the French. So…yes."

The idea was so large, and so unrelated to Hill 881, that Joe remained silent.

"I believe Robert Capa was the only European in our country who understood the situation there," Cuong said.

"How?"

"His anger at The French. His eastern European…the socialism. His being a Jew. He thought of the French as fascists defending a failed system." Cuong fell into a kind of flowing disappointment. "Vichy in Vietnam. Imagine thinking that arming the fortress at Dien Bien Phu had anything to do with the history of French civilization." He took in a breath. "You would think the people who fueled the Renaissance would know better."

"And what can *we* count on, Cuong, you and I? What is there that we can…can…."

"The two of us?"

"Yes."

Cuong remained silent…a long moment. "The flames."

Joe took in a breath.

"The fire." Cuong's utterance, like the memory of the flames themselves, caused in Joe a momentary seizure of terror, as his memories had so done so frequently. He contemplated the killing zone on 881, with its white, exploded phosphorous engulfing the bodies next to him, and shuddered with the realization, once more, as so often since that very moment, that his own musculature had itself been charred and in effect left behind in that hole, while his heart and mind had gone on.

"How do *you* think about the flames?" Joe said.

Cuong did not respond. He turned the paper cup, now only half filled with tea, about with his left hand. "I remember so little." He looked out to the pathway and, as Joe had, observed his granddaughter conversing with Samuel. "The flames are what I remember." He looked down, his left hand still caressing the paper cup. "The phosphorous. The napalm. And, like you, I thought afterwards about what it all meant, for good and bad. Your President Johnson. Your General Westmoreland. My Chairman Ho. My General Giap. All that. I read book after book. But what remains in my heart is the fire, Joe." He swallowed and sat back, lifting his eyes toward Joe's. His mouth tightened. He sighed, looking away. "The moment, after your M-16s, when I was crawling from those flames."

Joe saw that Samuel and Shirley had turned and were coming back to the boathouse.

"The terrible choking," Cuong said.

That the two physicians had so much expertise in their field, and yet appeared so much like a tableau of the 20th and the 21st centuries chatting together, decades apart, youth and age, east and west, fresh learning versus weathered knowledge....

"The choking." Cuong grimaced, looking away. "I'm sure you know that. It burned your lungs."

"Killed my friends," Joe said. *But this lake, this air, here, now*.... he thought. *We can breathe here.*

"And mine," Cuong said.

—

"You know, the wounded went on and strove for life, Joe." Samuel sat down, unbuttoning his suit coat as Shirley and Cuong walked the path toward their car. "Like you and Cuong. For yourselves and...the others. For their memory." He removed the panama and placed it on the table. "And I know your work helped bring you back." He moved the second piece of banana bread, still resting on the table in its wrap, back and forth before him. "I know that. Once you started writing, I knew that your studying..." He looked up and seemed startled to find his son so attentive to what he was saying. "...to be a doctor wouldn't have—"

"I *have* thought about that, you know."

"I hope so. It would have made me happy."

"I know, but—"

"Wait, though, Joey." Samuel studied the banana bread once more. "I think you're alive because you wrote about what happened."

"I do, too."

"Yeah, you lived it again, Joe." Samuel reached across the table and placed his hands over Joe's folded hands. "And it kept you—"

"Going."

"Yes. Your heart. That's what your books mean to me, Joey. It's your heart." He smiled. "It's the same for Shirley and her grandfather."

"How?"

"He's the reason she went to medical school." Samuel looked up. A kind of gathering together, an assertion of understanding, had entered his speech...a moment...a revealing.... "She understands his wounds."

BOBBY'S PIPER CUB

The clock was actually a model Piper Cub that Bobby Devlin had gotten as a birthday gift in 1944, when he was three.

The real Piper Cub airplane is now an antediluvian memory, manufactured so long ago that Bobby's granddaughter Flora would have to have researched it even when she was a girl. Just a moment ago, her mother Amelia had explained to her something about them, but in as few words as possible.

"The Piper Cub. It was an airplane," Amelia said.

"I can see that, Mother. But—"

"Popular when daddy was young."

The clock revealed that the Piper Cub had an enclosed cockpit. A single wing above the cockpit and a pair of tires extended from struts below it. Amelia explained that a real, full-grown Piper Cub went just seventy miles an hour. "I guess everyone liked them," she said. "It was small, slow, and, they say, popular. But they haven't made them for a long time." The clock itself was installed at the very front of the toy plane, a circular time piece with an hour hand, a minute hand, and a second hand placed just behind the propellor, run by a small battery inside, where the engine would have been in an actual Piper Cub. Except for the clock, this particular airplane, six inches long, was made of steel.

The clock was stopped.

Flora looked it over, top and bottom. Although because of the steel it was resistant to damage, she held it as though it were a fragile treasure.

With a reluctant whisper—"All right, if you insist." —her mother Amelia had opened the wooden box in which she had put the Piper Cub away many years ago, and handed it to Flora.

Bobby—Amelia's father—had died in a plane crash at the age of twenty-seven. Lieutenant JG Robert Devlin, U.S. Navy. Not in a Piper

Cub; rather in an A-4 Skyhawk trying to return to its base from a Marine Corps operation in an area called "The Market Place" in 1967. Flora knew the exact date of her grandfather's death. She had heard about it off and on from her mother Amelia all her life. For Amelia, the date was the central element in the obsession she had with her father's sudden abandonment of her. She had not forgiven him.

He had perished when the napalm still on his plane exploded as the A-4 plummeted into a field near which pinned down Marines had had to call for air cover. He had been hit by Vietnam People's Army rocket fire, something that almost never happened to Navy pilots. The rarity of such an event was another difficulty from which his daughter Amelia had not recovered.

Why him? Why then?

Amelia was reluctant to talk about the day she learned of his death, when she was four years old. Her mother Lydia had come out into the back garden where Amelia was digging in the ground with a trowel. Like Lydia, Amelia enjoyed gardening. She liked the dirt and the bugs. Flowers, when they emerged, thrilled the little girl. She remembered even now how the different colors engendered such pleasureful rushes of emotion in her. All of them warming, all sustaining…. Roses were pure excitement, especially deep red ones, and blue tulips calmed her down, so that reserve and thoughtfulness, not usually noted in four-year-olds, riffled through little Amelia whenever her mother picked some for her. And white camellias… pretty, sweet-minded…. She always examined them, always enjoyed them.

But her mother had been weeping when she came out of the house that day, and when she knelt down to take Amelia into her arms, the girl's surprise turned hurriedly to the wish to escape. Lydia's embrace made it difficult for Amelia to breathe.

"Oh, Amelia…your daddy…your daddy's…." Lydia had not been able to continue, and it was not until she escorted the little girl into the kitchen and lifted her onto a chair at the kitchen table, that Amelia learned of her father's fate. She did not understand it.

"Mommy? Daddy what?"

Small details of that scene remained with Amelia even now, when she was fifty-eight. The memory of her mother's weeping was like a rust-strewn blade, especially as Lydia had stood before the chair, isolated and distant from the four-year-old. So queried by Amelia, Lydia had broken down into sorrow and the abandonment of her little girl's question.

Amelia now lived on Telegraph Hill, on Lombard Street just below Coit Tower. Her daughter Flora's home was several blocks further down, nearer to the base of The Crooked Street. Mother and daughter had not gotten along very well…ever. Amelia had grown up believing that self-protection was the one thing that mattered, and that any deviation from that idea was to be censured…indeed, put down. Her daughter Flora's personality had seemed to Amelia proof that Flora just didn't get it. Flora was too pretty. Too loud. Too funny. And, especially, too smart. That Flora's school friends and, more important, her mother's social friends enjoyed those features of the girl's personality was clear to Amelia. Above all, Flora was too free. So, Amelia did what she could to tamp down her daughter's behavior. She was to be unsuccessful in that endeavor even into Flora's own motherhood and the evident happiness and adventurousness of *her* daughter Alice.

Flora occasionally dreamed about her grandfather. In the dreams a young boy, Bobby was reserved, always carefully dressed, a lover of ocean waves, handsome and fun. She suspected his wishes for her would thrum with kindness. In each dream she was a little girl herself and enjoyed walking the path to the Golden Gate Bridge with him when she cherished simply *being* with him, during which she could jump into the serene waves of the beach that runs along the bay by Crissy Field…even in winter, hand in hand with sweet-minded, luminous Bobby.

Although they had never met, Flora's father Mike sympathized with Bobby Devlin's wish to fly. An investment banker, he was himself a collector of books of every sort about flight. His collection covered the gamut from an illustrated small press edition of Da Vinci's flying machines through The Smithsonian's book *Aircraft,* a summation of the entire idea of manned flight. Mike owned about a hundred such titles. As a young man, he had planned to get a pilot's license, but his wooing of Amelia had brought an end to that. Respectful of Amelia's wishes, Mike had realized that one of them was based on the one true bitterness in her life: the death of her father. Before their wedding, Amelia made Mike promise not to fly, and Mike acquiesced because he so cared for her.

As their daughter Flora was growing up, Mike realized that the girl had something that he himself did not, which was an unstructured wish to spill her own feelings. Judging from what he knew of Bobby Devlin, Mike sensed that his daughter was probably a lot like Bobby. Flora seldom insisted on those feelings when she was with her mother, out of frustration with her. But Mike knew they were there, despite Amelia's efforts to keep Flora buttoned up.

Flora would not be buttoned.

And now, Flora's daughter Alice had no plans for being buttoned up herself. She was fifteen, a student at The Urban School. Her grades were good enough; if she kept going the way she always had, she would go to Stanford, Yale, or some such. She was a soccer player as well, and this summer worked out on evenings with guys on the football field at Galileo High School. Most there had played soccer in high schools and colleges, and even one or two on some kind of professional team. To eventually play at that level was the dream that brought Alice to Galileo High.

The first time Flora watched Alice there, she noted the preponderance of men on the field, and assumed they would want to discourage girls from playing with them. But early in the game, Flora saw how the other players were watching her play and, more important, were eventually starting to get the ball to her. Alice was not afraid to defend, either, and roughed up one of the opponent players during that first game. He even complained to her about it, getting into her face. Alice turned her back and waved a hand, smiling at him and muttering something like a cheerful "Get used to it, Pal."

Alice's plan was to go to The Olympics.

Flora was examining the Piper Cub. "Mother, it's been so long since I've seen this." Her smile offered a suggestion of familial glee. Amelia had forgotten she had hidden the wooden case on that closet shelf. She herself took the case down only every few years, to look over some of Bobby's letters. She had cherished certain ones, those in which her father had written about how much he missed his little girl Amelia. He wrote a graceful hand, very unlike what most men are capable of. The ease of reading his love letters to Lydia, written so carefully, was a special treat for Amelia. His handwriting made the clear affections in the letter even more special.

"I'm dreaming of your hair, Lydia, and how soft it is in my hands."

"Wasn't that room in Carmel something? The way we *inaugurated* it!"

"Please ask Amelia to think of me as much as she can. I feel it when she does. Believe me, I feel it!"

Amelia had seldom shared these letters with Flora, worried about what, of her own feelings, she would give away to her daughter: especially what she hated about Bobby's death. She had always insisted that Flora be guided through any such revelation and protected from it. But "guidance" actually meant "evasion." What Amelia hated, she kept sequestered. It was all Bobby's fault, and Amelia would keep that thought to herself because she cherished the purity of her own anger with her father. She was not about to give Bobby any slack in any of this. She kept how she felt to herself.

She kept it imprisoned.

Flora took a few letters from the case, which lay on the low living room table around which the three women sat. Lined in green felt, the case held about fifty of them. Her mother had kept them ordered by the dates on which they had been written. This neatness reminded Flora of Amelia's insistence that everything…everything…be organized. Dishes in their cabinets. Furniture each piece in its place. Her closet in sections of jackets, dresses, scarves, blouses…shoes…underwear…. *Her emotions, too,* Flora thought on occasion as she would remind herself of the silent rages…not always silent…of which her mother was capable, intended for her husband Mike, her daughter Flora, and especially the memory of her father Bobby and his betrayal of her.

For Flora, the real surprise in the box was the Piper Cub, which she had not seen in years. She turned it over to examine it. Etched into the top of the wing were the words "Piper Aircraft," and, below them, another, separate, etched inscription, this one dated. "For my little Amelia: Christmas, 1966. Daddy."

Flora imagined her mother as a girl in a party dress for Christmas. She had pictures of Amelia, a perfect blonde. Curled hair, ribbons, and Mary Janes. She knew there *must* have been such moments in little Amelia's life in which she *had* been able to luxuriate in simple joy. Flora had seen only occasional expressions of love as they emanated from her mother. Usually for kids other than Flora herself. Her two cousins Morrie and Steff, who still lived in Napa and had always been close friends with Flora. They were now brother and sister owners of a winery. Also, her gay actor cousin Ben, who had been a little too demonstrative for Amelia's taste, but whose theatrics as a kid nonetheless had amused her. Ben now had a stellar career going in New York. Jalen, who had grown up in San Francisco and had become a venture capitalist in London. A nice fellow. Tight-lipped, grumpy, but in the end okay. Rich. Mostly boys, in other words. Flora had missed out on getting the kinds of smiles the boys got from her mother. That those boys had found Flora herself to be such fun miffed Amelia, but, still, *because* they were boys, she was able to soften her resentment of Flora's popularity with them. Some things, Amelia knew, you can't control.

"Mom, did you read this one?" Alice held one of the letters. "Grandpa Bobby's so sweet!" Without a pause, she began reading it out loud. "'Tell little Amelia how much I love her. And please tell her this. I had the experience of flying upside down this morning. It was a training moment, in which they want you to be able to navigate upside down in case that state of things is ever imposed upon you in a combat situation. The training officer told us that this can be a difficult thing to do. 'You won't have experienced it,' he said. 'You won't be used to it.' But you know, Lydia, I loved it. Everything is backwards when you're upside down. It was fun. Tell Amelia that, please, because I bet she'd enjoy it. Fun!'"

Alice looked up, a smile on her face. "Gee, I'd *love* to feel that." But Amelia had lowered her head and a sigh burrowed from her now, despite her effort to block it. It floated like a disorganized smudge from her throat.

"Grandma?" Alice folded the letter and replaced it in the envelope. She was careful not to damage the envelope or the letter itself. Amelia remained silent, except for this emission of sadness. She swore at herself. She hated the sigh.

Alice addressed her once more…a near whisper. "Grandma?"

Flora moved to the loveseat and sat down next to Amelia. She put her arm around her mother's shoulders and pulled her close. She glanced toward Alice, who now appeared worried that she had done something awful. The envelope hung from her hand.

Amelia acquiesced to Flora's sympathy, leaning toward her. "Why didn't Daddy come back?" she whispered. Rapt pain flowed through her feelings. But after a few seconds, Amelia took Flora's hand from her shoulder and pushed it away. "Leave me alone."

Alice watched. Her sympathy with her grandmother's sadness was clear. Flora and Alice had seldom seen such expressiveness in Amelia. But, as in those moments when Amelia would put a stop to the tears, the sigh, or the dark silence, it was to be understood that this was *indeed* a stop. The straightened back, the determined intake of breath, and the abrupt change of subject to some observation—of what was on at the Asian Art Museum or with whom she was having tea tomorrow—would replace the self-examination. Alice *had* seen this. But she was less frustrated by it now than was her mother Flora, who had seen so much more of it.

"Mother, what does this little airplane mean to you?" Flora moved from the loveseat and sat down again on her own chair. She took up the Piper Cub. "Why have you kept it hidden?"

"None of your business, dear."

The "dear" was like a gate, closing.

"Mother!"

Alice gave a hurried glance at Flora.

"What does it mean to you, Mother?"

Alice had not seen her mother, ever, with so abrupt a tone of voice with *her* mother.

Amelia folded her hands on her lap. Her already white hair, still full, remained unbothered. Her blue eyes as well. Flora could feel the gathering resistance with which her mother so often fended off a display of emotion.

"Thoughtlessness, dear."

"Thoughtlessness! Whose? Yours?"

"His!" Amelia said.

"Grandpa?"

"All he cared for was himself. For that airplane, that…whatever it was…that foolish Vietnam of his." Amelia's eyes took in Alice's hands and the letter. "Upside down! How can a man who suffered the way he must have…."

Alice sat back, now appearing even more guilty than before. "Oh, Grandma, I didn't—"

"Be quiet, Alice." Amelia's lips tightened. She looked down.

Alice's straight black hair, quite long, only partially hid her face. Her own lips appeared forced together, two tight straps.

"Leave Alice alone, Mother," Flora said.

Amelia looked up.

"You think Grandpa Bobby was just some kind of kid?"

"No, dear. He was a lieutenant JG in the—"

"What you just did, *that's* what thoughtlessness is, Mother!" Flora took the envelope from Alice. "You leave Alice alone!" She placed the envelope back in the box. "And anyway, what do you think Grandpa's death was, a lark?"

"Flora. This isn't any of your—"

"It is too my business. He was my grandfather."

"Maybe so, dear. But he was my—"

"Mother!"

Amelia took up her cup of tea. She felt her heart folding inside, as though it wished to hide away undiscovered…undiscoverable. She had watched Flora's enjoyment of the Piper Cub and now recalled how she too had protected the little airplane whenever she examined it. By herself. In her bedroom.

A secret joy.

"I'm sorry, Mother." Flora lowered her eyes. Angry with herself for the outburst, she was contrite, as though she had, yet again, crossed the barrier that had always been so resistant to attack…even kindly attack. She was asking herself, yet once more, why she even tried.

Amelia determined to do nothing about Flora's kindness. She understood her own jealousy of her daughter, which had led almost always to continued disaffection. But Amelia now noticed Alice's concern for *her* mother, and realized the girl thought Flora was being victimized. Attacked. Amelia had not ever recognized these exchanges as victimization, at least consciously. She treated Flora the way she did in order to protect her. She could not imagine that Flora would understand the devastation she herself felt even now, so many years after her father's terrifying death. Why *didn't* Daddy come back? Why did his derring-do seem, as it had ever since Amelia had been capable of thinking about such things, like self-killing treachery?

Amelia had often imagined Bobby's death. He went to it despite his daughter's love for him. *He forgot all about me.* She dwelt on the pain of the napalm incinerating him.

She rushed to push the thought aside, although it was yet another version of the same suspicion that had run through her mind hundreds of times. Reason told her to stop this and to forgive Bobby. But the instantaneous flash, the flames, the explosion engulfing him….

"Flora?"

Flora grimaced.

"Alice, please ask your mother to…"

Alice waited as Amelia took in a breath.

"Alice….to take the Piper Cub with her. To take it home."

Flora glanced at Alice, who took the envelope and its letter from the box.

 "Grandma?" Alice said.

"Yes. You can keep the letter."

"Mother?" Flora held the Piper Cub in her right hand.

"Care for them, that's all I ask, Flora. Alice. Care for them, and…."

Flora thought she was about to witness her mother's retreat into regretful anger, which was usually the final touch to any fractious conversation they may have been having. But this, now…. Usually, her mother would be in retreat. Going into hiding.

"Think of Daddy," Amelia said. Her half-hidden eyes offered a moment of actual sincerity. Her wish for his love…. "And, now and then, of me." She waited a moment. "I know how much you would have loved him, both of you." Amelia swallowed and took in a breath. "Even though you never…."

She took up the box from the table and examined it a moment in silence.

She placed it on her lap and caressed the top of it, her fingers light against its varnished grain. As a teenager at Sacred Heart High School, Amelia had brought out the Piper Cub every few months just to hold it and to think about how thoughtful it proved her father to have been…his last act of kindness to his daughter before he perished. As she got older, she had to do combat with her anger with Bobby and his stupid navy and his dumb A4 whatever-it-was. During those times, she would take the Piper Cub into her hands, turn the little plane around in her fingers to examine it, and try imagining her father taking her up in it…to fly over the bay so she could watch the silk-driven sailboats, or out over the ocean above the sun-brightened doorway of the Golden Gate bridge, or across the green-dew hills of Marin County, its surging farmlands and fog-seeking forests.

"Even though you never had the joy of loving him," Amelia said.

NONO

There were moments in which Mike did not understand Mimi. Some weeks ago, they had been rehearsing a particular move, and Mimi couldn't get it. The simplest of tango motions, in which the follower is given the opportunity to lift her back foot slightly off the floor behind her, give it a little dissociated flourish, and then bring it forward and across, to be placed lightly—the very tip of it—by the side of the other, planted, foot.

It was a stylish period offered at the end of a delicate sentence.

But Mimi couldn't get it.

"Well, listen, Mike, lead it better," she said after the fifth misapplication.

Mimi had accepted Mike's invitation to be his partner for the upcoming *La Pista Porteña*, a competition in San Francisco (their first such together), even though, when he asked her, he had felt insecure in his own abilities. After years of tango, he still worried that he was too Anglo-Saxon to essay the dance successfully, especially in an international contest being judged by…by an Argentine! There is about the dance a kind of unspoken requirement that you be at least Argentine, and even more so a Buenos Aires *porteño*, in order to do it well. An Uruguayan *oriental* from Montevideo too, if that's what you're stuck with. And there would be a number of immigrant *porteños* and *orientales* competing in this very contest.

The judge was to be El Olvidado, a *tanguero* on tour in the United States just now, who was noted for his lovely traditional tango and its slow beauties. *The New York Times* had raved about him.

Mike's insecurities had little to do with the mechanics of the dance and a great deal to do with the histories of mass immigration to Buenos Aires and Montevideo, the explosive finesse of west-African rhythms in both, and the benighted sorrows of Mediterranean-style betrayal and lost love that so flower in both capitols. These issues do not figure for much if you are a New England Protestant *gringo*, which Mike was.

He was nonetheless congratulated for his dance. He could do it. But even he knew that, by comparison to the *compadres* of the Rio de La Plata, he was a little on the wooden side.

Mimi too suffered, but for different reasons. Her unreasonable beauty put the lie to her signature talents as the director of technology of a San Francisco accounting software startup. She had a mind devoted to strict necessity. Mimi never forgot anything. Having led the design team for the software, and then been involved with selling it to places like Deutsche Bank, she approached most things with a sense of well thought-out, singular organization.

But her looks occasionally got in the way, the banker on the other side of the table being a little too forward for her to complete her presentation of the software's benefits. If she herself were perceived of as the benefit, she had to become difficult in order to get him off her case and to close the deal. There is a danger in this, too, since being difficult doesn't usually result in a sale.

That tango has so little to do with software was one of the principal reasons Mimi loved it. On the dance floor, she could let her grace and sensuality flower. It was the music. And tango offers lush movement that no business endeavor can even attempt. Mimi nonetheless looked for precision in her dance, despite the fact that so much of what tango offers has to do with erotic splendor. Perhaps, though, tango's benefits were actually the very starting point for Mimi's singularity in the dance, the ones that enabled her…rather, compelled her…to put on the dance pumps and to step marvelously into Mike's arms. Tango wove itself in with Mimi's lovely display. It threaded her movements with invitation, her emotional intensities with desire, however little that had to do with the spreadsheets she had invented.

Mike knew about spreadsheets. He was an attorney who helped California start-ups with their business-founding legal work. Curt, the principal partner of his firm, was a Yale graduate whose emotional thinness caused Mike to think of him as Absence in a school tie. He wanted to see only those spreadsheets that celebrated the financial success of his firm's clients. He just glanced at those that showed ineptitude. Curt wanted to appear kindly and approachable, and told all his attorneys and even his employees to use his first name, although privately they grumbled about his ignoring them every chance he got. One day he criticized Mike for the numbers of one of his clients. Curt was on the board of that particular client. "It doesn't show in the spreadsheets, Mike, so you'd better get on it!" This was unjust, and Mike protested. "Get on it!" Curt insisted, absently.

"You ask me to do something," Mimi now said, stepping away from Mike. "I do it. And then you criticize me for it."

"Mimi!"

"No! That's what you do."

"I do not."

"You do, too."

This quibbling between them was not new. They had found that, although each had been dancing for some years, even in Buenos Aires dancehalls, each felt the other was too demanding. Neither ever stumbled. They even had a certain showy *joie de vivre* that made their dance special. But the sense each had of his or her own wishes for tango caused them now and then to stumble emotionally. The footwork was okay. It was their hurt feelings that tripped them up.

"Look…can we work this out?" Mike said.

Mimi did realize that insisting only on your own point of view in tango is an open door to bad dancing. So, despite wanting to bop him one, Mimi allowed the wish to fester alone inside her heart, because she sensed that Mike really hoped they could meet each other on this issue. Their tango would suffer without it.

"Yes, we *can* work it out, Mike."

"Okay. Good. So, try following—"

"No, no. You just lead it. I'll follow."

They soldiered on.

Two weeks before the competition, they met El Olvidado.

They had attended a show he had choreographed and was starring in, at the Alcazar Theater on Geary Street. *¡El destino en sí!* which is to say *Fate Itself!* El Olvidado was the principal dancer, with two other fellows and three *porteñas,* all of whom were superb. He had six fine musicians, also. Nonetheless, the show featured the usual inanities that so many producers feel are *de rigueur* in staged tango: the whole thing takes place in a whorehouse; the knife fight scene between two *macho* petty gangsters; the testosterone-driven dance competition among all the petty gangsters, *mano a mano;* the insolent resentment, on the part of the chief petty gangster, of the pretty prostitute's sensuous indifference....

And much more.

Mike seldom went to such shows anymore because they are all alike, one to the next. He sensed that the producers of Argentine tango shows *must* be capable of deeper feelings than those exhibited in so much repetitive cliché. But he had not seen it. Once, a few years ago, when he had asked one of the dancers at another show why they all seemed to cherish these roles, and to dance them over and over, the fellow told him *"Che ¡es tango!"* Mike didn't believe it. That wasn't tango. Rather than the complicated heart of a difficult dance, it was the sorry display of plain raggedy *machismo.* The music is so varied and complicated, and the emotional commitment you have to make if you're going to dance it at all so encompassing, that the "petty gangster" gig on stage is really just a comma in what is, given all of tango's history, a massive classic novel.

—

El Olvidado showed up at the dance studio where Mike and Mimi practiced. His being gorgeous as well as famous, Mimi noticed him right away. About forty, slim with very straight and very black hair, with a finely formed chin that, if anything, enhanced the authority of his glance, he looked the petty gangster part himself even as he stepped in quiet toward a folding metal chair to the side of the dance studio. The part about being "petty" seemed immediately inaccurate. As he sat down, dropping his shoulder bag to the floor, he appeared, just settling and arranging himself, capable of heart-engaged passion.

He watched Mimi and Mike dance.

A moment later, they introduced themselves, telling Olvidado that they had seen his show.

"What's your real name?" Mimi asked.

"They call me Olvidado, yes," he said. "But I am Nono Bianchi."

"Bianchi?"

"Yes." Olvidado grinned. "Like the racing bicycle." He turned his head to the side, lifting his large chin so that he could give the two dancers an impressive profile. "But no relation." He leaned his head to the side, offering Mimi another smile.

"Then why El Olvidado?" Mike asked. "The Forgotten One."

"Tango," Olvidado said.

"How so?"

"It is a lost art. Disappeared…I mean, the way it was. The street corner. The poor young men. The immigrants. The *boliche*. The *conventillo*."

Mike translated. "A *boliche,* Mimi, is like a little store or tavern, a tango dive, and a *conventillo* was a large Buenos Aires building that housed immigrants from all over. 1890s. Early 1900s."

"Yes," Olvidado said. "And tango, of course, came from both those places." He sat back on the chair and sighed.

"So…they're *olvidado?"* Mike said.

"Quite forgotten. For tango, those were the long ago. With my great-grandfather Juanito, who lived in a *conventillo* as a young man and danced in *boliches*."

"A dancer?" Mimi said.

"*Sí ¡Y era fantástico, amor!"* Olvidado shrugged. "At least, according to my grandmother. She danced with him when she was a girl." He folded his hands and examined them. A look of saddened nostalgia took him over. "Those were the romantic times." His face took on the appearance of a Goya peasant, drawn in swathes of grey and black. Passion and grit themselves. There was in it a sense of great loss, as though the times of which he was speaking were now so gone in distant memory that only a few people these days could conjure them up. The great tragedy of tango. The soul of it…disappeared. Replaced by emptiness. Lost in mere nostalgia.

Mike noticed the look of bereavement that Olvidado gave to Mimi.

Olvidado stood up and took her into his arms. Mimi was surprised and resisted, although only for a moment. Quite soon, she gave in to him. "My great-grandfather held his daughter like this, you see." Mike could tell that, given the ease and grace with which Mimi essayed a few steps with the Argentine, the Argentine well knew what he was doing. "Authority, but respect." They danced an entire tango that was so slow that the exchange reminded Mike of sad fluidity itself, especially on Mimi's part. Once the music meandered to its end, Olvidado escorted her back toward the chair, releasing her hand. "And grace, of course." He glanced toward Mike. "*Con permiso…*" He gave him a slight nod and a grin that implied he was making fun of him. "*…maestro.*"

Olvidado watched Mike and Mimi dance a few numbers, and then advised them. Mike felt he was being observed by some actor playing a dark role deepened by imminent danger.

The godfather.

At first, Mimi was even more nervous than Mike. But after a few suggestions from Olvidado, during which he formed and caressed the part of her frame that he wished to correct, she seemed to have softened and found new peacefulness. A lot of peacefulness, it seemed to Mike.

"Your back, Mimi," Olvidado observed at one moment. "It is lovely."

—

"Watch out for him."

Mimi surveyed the glass of wine before her.

"These kinds of guys are famous in Buenos Aires."

"None of your business." She caressed the rim of the glass, studying it.

"Mimi, I—"

"You're not my chaperon."

"Yes, but we know women, you and I—we do!—who've been used by men like him."

"Maybe *you* do. I like him."

"Of course! He *intends* for you to like him, Mimi."

"Mike!"

"He does!"

—

They danced in *La Pista Porteña*...and Olvidado gave them the win. The applause was noisy and convinced Mike after a few minutes that indeed he and Mimi *had* excelled. There were two Argentine couples in the competition and one couple from Montevideo. All these kept their congratulations of Mike and Mimi in reserve, and one of the Argentine men actually scowled at them as they took the floor for a post-celebration solo turn for the audience's benefit. Mike knew the Argentine...a San Francisco wine merchant named Paco Odónaju, often called "Irlandés" by Argentine friends. Mike had known Paco for some years and had never had a successful conversation with him. Paco seemed to think that all *yanqui boludos* who even attempted tango were laughable. He was a fine dancer riven with jealous anger.

Mimi went out with Olvidado the next evening. They were going for dinner because, she told Mike, "he's got some kind of proposal in mind."

"A date? An affair?"

"Mike! Please!"

This inquiry of Mike's surprised him as well. He had thought of Mimi as simply a dance partner. Before their relationship, he had danced with her off and on at *milongas*...nothing serious. He had kept his emotional distance, realizing how good a dancer she was and not wishing to turn his feelings for her, or hers for him, into anything more than professional regard. Even then, Mike had *La Pista Porteña* in mind, and knew that he had to keep his eyes on the contest. And although they did have regard, they were not professionals or anything close to it; rather, devotees of the dance and the music. Certainly not of each other.

That is, until this moment....

Mike stuck his hands in his pants pockets and turned to the side, fighting off the scowl that wished to appear on his lips.

She phoned him the next day and cancelled their plan to dance later in the afternoon. "Olvidado's got some things he wants to teach me."

"Tango things." Mike was jealous.

"Of course."

"Nothing else."

"Mike."

Having finished the conversation with greying good-byes, Mike sat back in his chair and realized what was happening. He cared for Mimi, suddenly without warning and seemingly unaware of the possibility—until now clueless of its own existence—that he may be in love her.

—

Mimi invited Olvidado for coffee.

She lived in The Marina, just a block from The Marina Green and its views of the bay and of Alcatraz itself. Mike had explained to her that in Spanish an *alcatraz* is a kind of seabird...a gannet, he had read. But maybe the Spanish explorer Juan Manuel de Ayala had mistaken west coast seagulls for east coast gannets, which de Ayala would have been able to see only if he had discovered Penobscot Bay instead of San Francisco Bay. In any case, Mike had assumed that the island had once been a haven for seagulls, before it became the other kind of haven for which it is now so famous. He had visited Alcatraz a few times in his life and recalled seeing only occasional seagulls. They seemed no longer to go to the island for more than a startled glimpse of it.

"You enjoy it here?" Olvidado looked around the living room. He was dressed in a white shirt and khaki pants, a white tennis sweater resting about his shoulders, the sleeves in a loose knot on his chest. The red and blue stripes that bordered the neck of the sweater seemed to accentuate his square jaw and lovely eyes. He also wore a pair of black leather loafers with no socks. His southern Italian coloring made even his ankles appear alluring to Mimi.

Because of her business success, her apartment was a luxury. It was so well appointed that it had become the location of choice for her company for entertaining visiting clients. Although many software engineers have suddenly come into the kinds of money that would allow luxury like

Mimi's, few would understand the difference between the fine accoutrements in her kitchen and their own now dented and blackened pots and pans, the coffee-stained mug and so on, all bought a few years ago at Ikea.

Mimi was still without real love after ten years in software development. The other engineers where she had worked during that time had given her all the engineer-speak she ever needed, not a syllable of it thoughtful. Love's language was so much more subtle than that provided by binary systems, no matter how many zeroes and ones and no matter in whatever combination of them.

She led Olvidado into the kitchen and began preparing coffee. She also brought out a few pastries from a bakery she loved named "Crusts of Bread and Such": a citrus morning bun that was her favorite of all their goods, and one of their croissants, which she thought were the best she had ever had, even among those her mother had bought for her in Paris when Mimi was fourteen and on her first ever trip outside the United States.

She knew that software engineers know nothing about croissants.

"I do like it, yes," she said to Olvidado. "We're so lucky that we live in San Francisco."

"I have danced in Oakland, across the bay. It is no San Francisco." Olvidado fingered the croissant. "But you know that, I am sure."

"I was born in Oakland."

"Ay!" Olvidado removed his fingers from the pastry. "I am sorry. I mean no—"

"Don't worry. San Francisco is in a league of its own."

Olvidado broke into a large smile. *"Che, como Buenos Aires ¿non?"*

After coffee, he asked her to dance. They pulled aside the rug in Mimi's living room, and Olvidado put Mimi through three of the most delicious tangos she had ever experienced. After that, they went for a walk that took them toward the Golden Gate Bridge, on the trail that borders the bay. The blue sky was enlivened by the whitest of clouds. The bay itself reflected the sky with a dark cerulean calm seldom experienced here, where wind is almost constant. But, on this day, no…and Mimi felt that the quiet that fell across the waters formed a kind of expectant listening to her conversation with Olvidado, in hopes of an affectionate revelation.

Actually, Mimi tried to put that notion aside because she knew that Mike was right about a certain kind of Buenos Aires *tanguero*. Among the women dancers in North and South America, Europe, and Asia...everywhere...they are well known and numerous. They flaunt their talent in the ways of pretty birds in search of a mate. She did know women who had fallen for this, and most of them had decided that they had been fools, once the pretty birds had escaped with some of their money. Or if not their money, a good deal of their virtue, which had been abandoned in expectation of what they feel must be the superior ability of such men to put women into ecstasy itself. This turns out not necessarily to be true. But the expectation opens the door for just enough time for the pretty bird to put his sensuous talents into action, such as they may be.

After that, he's gone.

But she was attracted to him. His English was formal, well-spoken, clear, and considerate. He asked her questions, and then listened to her answers. He offered little of the bony, obdurate insistence upon themselves that so many men seem to think is interesting to women. Although, when it was Olvidado doing that, it *was* interesting. His smoothness, about which Mike had warned Mimi, was for her a plus. It seemed so genuine, especially when it thrilled her expectations. He seemed more complete than any of her work compatriots, although she realized...once again and sadly...that the men she worked with were as incomplete as you can get emotionally. She knew that they *had* to have emotions. But the stumbling that was the feature of their response to any question that begins with the phrase "How do you feel about..." was what sufficed for language until they could get back to the matters at hand: sets of numbers, the mouse versus the touchpad, the next round of funding....

They left the trail for a moment to walk out onto the beach that it borders. On such days as this, the beach is crowded mostly with young parents and their kids. It is a celebration for all, including the many dogs that run up and down, into and out of the water, their noise and happiness enjoyed by the kids themselves as they dig in the sand or splash their toes in the small waves. The Golden Gate holds court over it all.

Mimi stumbled on one of the small boulders on which they were walking to get to the beach, and Olvidado took her hand. When she got her balance, he kept hold of her hand, and Mimi did not object.

The following day, Mimi spoke only of steps and combinations as she and Mike practiced. He hovered around questions of her time with Olvidado, but did not actually voice them. Mimi didn't bring up her stroll with Olvidado either. For a full hour, as they danced and talked, it was as if the stroll had not taken place. And, of course, there was nothing in the conversation about what Mimi and Olvidado did when they arrived back at her apartment, after the stroll.

—

Mimi threw a party for Olvidado. She invited Mike and many of the people with whom they danced tango. She also invited a few of the people from her company and, on a whim, two of the venture capitalists who had funded the company.

After a while, she addressed the guests. "And now my very dear friend Nono has asked me to dance with him."

Olvidado, standing behind her, his arms crossed, smirked.

Mike looked away. *Nono?*

"Professionally he is known as El Olvidado," Mimi said. "And has danced tango everywhere in the world."

Nono!

With the exception of Mike, Nono was the only man among the guests who wore a tie. Mimi knew that these days, as a fashion item, ties are out. She hadn't liked this change, thinking that a tie brings great style to a man, no matter the state of the rest of his dress. Even a fine Uomo suit looks everyday if it is not accompanied by a proper tie. One of the things she had asked Mike to do when they danced at the *milongas* was to wear one, and to her surprised pleasure he always did.

The tangos Mimi and Nono danced stunned the onlookers. Especially Mike. Grumbling to himself, he had moved to the end of one of the couches, folded his arms, and leaned against the wall. He hoped he did not have a scowl on his face, but he did. He was hurt. And the dance he witnessed served only to enflame his wishes for Mimi.

Nono moved like the roué everyone in the room concluded he was. He was dark and thoughtful, his walking like that of a graceful, intimate lover intent on enhancing his partner's very beauty. Mimi was no slouch either and bore no resemblance to the women in Nono's stage show. Her silk dress flowed about her like a gold and silver cloud. Her shoes, barely held to her feet by slim straps, were quite high-heeled and formed an extension of her legs that made her pretty feet breathtaking. Her dark hair, which was long, sometimes hid her eyes, which could be seen especially when they were half-hidden by it, their lashes curving with happiness.

Mike looked around the living room. Even the software engineers were interested.

Afterwards, Nono engaged the venture capitalists in talk. Both were men, and both carried themselves with aggressive self-admiration. His dancing may have impressed these fellows. But now, he spoke with them with the meaty gestures, the grudging confidence, and the blunt dismissals with which such men converse with each other. Like them, he had no wish to appear a flake. Even were he not a streetwise *tanguero*, Nono now had at least the appearance of a fearless venture capitalist himself, one of no doubt great notoriety in rough-and-tumble, ever-rising South America.

But Mike also noticed, when Mimi brought around a plate of hors d'oeuvres, that while these men offered congratulations to her for her dancing and smiled manfully at her obvious beauty, they paid her little real attention. Mike knew why: she simply was not one of them, and there was a reason for that. Her talents as an executive in the start-up were well known. But in the end, these fellows acted toward her as though some fellow could do just as good a job. Their thanks for a damp, cold shrimp dipped in lumpy cocktail sauce reeked of indifference. And, to Mike's astonishment, their polite arrogance toward Mimi was acquiesced to by Nono himself. He seemed actually to urge the arrogance, so that they could bore Mimi and then get back to what he wished to talk about.

—

Fate Itself! was extended for three weeks at The Alcazar. With the three-day break asked for from the producers, Nono and Mimi motored in her BMW to the Napa Valley.

Mike took this opportunity to fall into despondency. Now, finally, he realized how much he wished for Mimi and the gristle and wonder of real love. He realized what she could mean to him. There was no equal for Mike to holding Mimi in his arms while being serenaded by tango. Where before they had maintained the emotional distance from each other, having the dance be the enjoyment, the *Pista Porteña* in view…now Mike realized that dancing with Mimi was not the end in itself. Love was the end. The dance was its vehicle. And now, even the vehicle was gone.

—

"Mimi, that is not what you should do." Nono stepped away from her, turning his back as he brought the fingers of his right hand to his lips. The gesture implied glum self-importance. "You do not see what I am trying to give you."

"Of course I do, Nono."

"It is easy."

"Nono."

"It is easy!"

"Well, listen, Nono, lead it better."

—

Mimi called Mike, and he invited her for coffee on Chestnut Street, a few blocks from her apartment. He knew that Nono had moved in with Mimi for the duration of *Fate Itself!* and he had not heard from her. The phone call came as a surprise. But Mike made the invitation immediately.

They sat down at a table before the café. It was a warm morning, and the umbrella that shaded them served to obscure the lines of worry that had appeared around her eyes. Mike noted them but held back from any questions. She wore a pair of black slacks, a dark brown, long-sleeved silk blouse, a brooch that had a single pearl attached to the center of a sun-like circle of gold, and conservative black business heels.

"I've got to be in the office in an hour," she said. She sipped from her chamomile tea. "But I need to talk with you, Mike."

"Of course. What's happening?"

"Nono."

The pause that ensued was intentional on Mike's part. Right away he wished to celebrate. But given Mimi's worry lines, he felt that glee wouldn't be exactly the right response to her murmur of anguish. And Mike saw right away that this *was* anguish.

"I thought he was the man I'd been seeking…you know, for all those years up to the moment he asked me to dance." Mimi's hands rushed about one another as she stared at them. "And in that dance, I felt he *was* it." She lowered her head.

"What's the problem?"

"Tango."

"Tango's the problem?"

She frowned. "No. But it's the cause of the problem. I thought that…." She took in a breath, and then moaned. "Anyone who could dance like that…anyone who knows what it takes to dance like that…the personal sorrow and command that it requires—"

"All that."

"Yes! I thought a man like that was, you know, *the* man."

Mike sat back and looked out onto Chestnut Street. He realized that even he had misjudged Mimi. Yes, she danced better than anyone with whom he had ever danced. She moved with every intention of precision and grace. Her dance had no uncertain questions in it. But it was clear now to Mike that Mimi was a romantic, and that her sense of herself and her own value had been clouded by her expectations of Nono.

"How is it that he's not the man?" Mike said.

The cookies they had intended to share lay untested on their white ceramic plate. Mimi unbuttoned a sleeve of her blouse and rolled it up to her elbow. A dark blue and brown bruise splotched her forearm.

"He hit me."

Mike sat back. He stared at Mimi.

"He doesn't like me to criticize him."

"Do you?"

Mimi looked out on to the street herself. She let out a long breath. "If suggesting ways that he could dance better—"

"You do that with…El Olvidado?"

"I mean, that he could dance better with me."

"You do that?"

The skin just above and below her lips became finely wrinkled. "Actually, he's hit me a couple of times." Mimi placed a hand on her right shoulder and caressed it. This was the first time Mike had ever seen her lose the sense of her own appearance. He saw defeat. He saw rage.

"He kicked me."

"What?"

"He pushed me and I fell down…you know, in my living room. We were dancing."

"What had happened."

"I had bitched at him because he wouldn't leave me alone."

"About what?"

"About how I was dancing."

"And how *were* you dancing?"

Mimi slumped even more. "The way I always do. You know. With attention!"

"Verve."

"I hope so."

"Grace."

She now smiled, although with shyness and pain. "Thank you." Mike knew she hated telling him all this. But he also sensed that he may be the only person she trusted in a matter like this one.

"He kicked me here." She pointed to her right thigh and grimaced. "He was all apologies after that. All sad remorse."

"And you?"

"I didn't buy it." Mimi slouched. "Of course, I didn't buy it."

"I wouldn't think so."

Mimi brought her hands to her face and, after a moment, dropped them to her lap. She lowered her head.

"But can you prove it?"

"That he did all this?" Mimi swallowed, looking away.

"Yes. Any witnesses?"

The silence in their conversation was invaded by the laughter of passersby on the sidewalk, the wordplay and patter of women and their teenage daughters, the passage of small children, hands held by their fathers or guided along on their tricycles by their mothers....

"I installed those little cameras," she said.

"Cameras?"

"When I bought the place. The real estate guy said I should…you know, in case anybody broke in."

"Could we take a look?"

Mimi shrugged. "I guess. If I can figure out whether they work."

—

"Get the right attorney, Mike."

He had called a friend of his, Steven Abajian. They had been in the same class at Boalt Hall in Berkeley. A criminal lawyer, Steven's specialty was the defense of rock stars and Hollywood actors in drug cases. He had had many cases but was famous for those he had won. He once told Mike that he preferred defending black musicians because he understood that they had been arrested for being black, while the white musicians were arrested because they were foolish. It was easier to get a white musician or actor freed. But the defense of a black musician involved that musician's civil rights, which, although a civil rights case brought in less money, enabled Steven to work with people who were truly being victimized and whose work he deeply admired. Besides his street-cred, Steven Abajian had significant appreciation of stagecraft and musicianship.

He was a large man who seemed always to be lost in thought, even when telling stories about his past cases, which was often. Stocky, slovenly (although always wearing a tie), dressed in enormous, wrinkled suits, he had become a wealthy man. Mike enjoyed conversations with him because the people Steven represented were so often well-known, and the issues in their cases were so colorful, that few other attorneys in town could match him for anecdotal detail.

"Will *you* talk to Mimi, Steven?"

"Yeah. Have her call me." Steven nodded. He grumbled, a deep re-arrangement of phlegm in his throat, and placed the fingers of one of his hands against his lips. He looked up. "She won't ask me to dance, will she?"

—

It was the final night of *Fate Itself!* The theater was jammed, and in the last number, Nono did a spirited romantic turn with all three of the women in the cast. Each sequence brought a wave of applause, and when the musicians came to their final chord and the six dancers effected the usual photogenic poses that one always sees in pictures of tango dancers…the dark certainty of the men, the prideful disrespect of the women, all in poses of great corporeal superiority, their faces locked in self-assurance…the audience broke into stupendous clapping and noise. They came to their feet and cheered. In the curtain calls, Nono particularly received loud congratulation, and he returned the favor to the audience, smiling with broad intelligence and clapping for them.

As he walked from the stage, pounding one of the other fellows on the back and congratulating him, he was greeted by three policemen.

"Mr. Bianchi?" one of them said.

"Uh…*bueno*… ".

"Nono?"

"*Sí*. Yes."

"You're under arrest, sir."

"Arrest!"

'Yep. Battery. Assault."

"But—"

"You'll need to come with us, sir."

"But I—"

"Now!"

Mike and Steven Abajian were off-stage, standing back against a rear wall, next to a hanging, folded-up fire hose. As Nono shook his head and demanded to speak with his lawyer, one of the policemen read him his rights. Nono referred to this fellow and his fellow cops as *malditos pelotudos* until, finally, he was pushed out the stage door into the dank alley outside, where a fog-shrouded squad car awaited him. Steven nodded and offered a handshake to Mike. Mike apologized and pointed out that he was just now tapping in a number on his phone. Steven, of course, understood.

When Mimi answered, her voice was tremulous. When he told her the news, after a pained sigh, she thanked him. "Yes." There was a silence. "From my heart, Mike." She let out another sigh. "My very heart." Mike took in a breath and held it for a short moment until Mimi spoke again. "Yes."

CRUSTS OF BREAD & SUCH

Teetering as it does on the edge of the continent, San Francisco seemed fragile to Reggie. And when he read in the book before him about the 1906 earthquake, he realized his own airy insignificance. He looked out the window onto Columbus Avenue. You could die in an instant even here at City Lights. So quiet, the customers so respectful of where they are, the soft chaos of the John Coltrane tune playing throughout, the books like well-informed secrets…. Reggie had made this bookstore his go-to destination whenever he himself could not figure out what to do.

He was suffering from what he called "baker's blues," a condition that often throttled him. He couldn't get the chocolate coffee cake he had been thinking about to the point where the mix of ingredients would simply take command and the denouement would at last appear on the horizon. Reggie had so far come up with many solutions intended to usher him to that coffee cake moment, and none had succeeded.

He hated the phrase running through his head: *This isn't it, Reggie!* So, here in the bookstore, he thumbed through one book after another, replaced each on its shelf between its neighbors, and looked for yet one more. *All you need is a line…an encouragement*, he thought. Individual books had aided him before when his inventiveness wasn't working. But now…now…. These open pages, filled with runes, held not a clue. Not in this book. Not in any of them. The searched-for line needn't even mention chocolate or any other ingredient. What Reggie was looking for was the startling phrase that would dazzle him and let him know that he had better get back to the kitchen and get on with it.

For an example, the line "His soul had approached that region where dwell the vast hosts of the dead." Reggie was the only baker he knew who had even heard of *Dubliners*. The swirl of spirits in that line, the tempestuous accounting of death's enormity, had led him to more than one specific successful creation in his kitchen. The language sparked Reggie's own significant creativity.

"The vast hosts…." "The dead…." *Rhymes with bread,* he thought.

He left City Lights, knowing that he had to get home. He needed sleep and was due at work the following morning at three. The chief baker at Crusts of Bread & Such on Taylor Street in The Tenderloin, he and his assistant Josephine were working on a new possibility, a kind of chocolate-imbued pastry that was rolled and shaped into a loaf, so that the customer could cut it into thick slices, warm it, and baptize it with fine butter. Reggie knew that, when they got to the point of being able to sell it, it would be beyond delectable.

But they weren't there yet.

Getting off the 90 all-night Van Ness bus the next morning, he walked up the alley that would bring him to the bakery's side door. Even though it was so early, the alley was alive with conversation. There were bedraggled, stained tents on both sidewalks, and a number of residents jiving back and forth with each other, with considerable laughter here and there, and just as noisy complaint that was shouted out and shouted once more and then again by some crazy person.

Reggie knew several of these residents and was hailed by a few as he passed by. Some had flashlights. There were even lanterns in a few of the tents. He felt no danger, although he hurried up the alley, intent on the bakery. He felt he and Josephine were in the final stages of the new coffee cake, but before that, he had to get the crew going on all the other breads, pastries, and cookies. Josephine had suggested a different mixture of chocolate the morning before, with less sweetness, and as Reggie had thought about it at the bookstore, the idea became a revelation. He understood Josephine's description of how a slightly altered chocolate—a touch of raw Mexican and some distinguished French—could be enriched by Irish butter—not American—maybe with a bit more sea salt, to such a degree that the customer would wish to buy a whole coffee cake after having just a bite from one slice.

When he got to the bakery, he looked back up the alley and saw a narrow, semi-destroyed village, mess scattered everywhere. *Perhaps,* he thought, *like the rest of the world will be after global warming.*

He entered Crusts of Bread & Such.

By nine a.m., Josephine's suggestion had worked. They had put a loaf together as she had described it, tested and baked it. With a cup of coffee before each of them in the café itself, seated at the large main window in front, they sampled a slice without butter, and then one with. Both were superb, and each enhanced the coffee. As they shook hands across the table, Reggie congratulated Josephine. She had come into the café as a mere front-counter attendant some months ago and had voiced a wish to be trained as a baker. Reggie had promoted her after several requests and much insistence, and now realized what a mistake it would have been not to do so.

A few hours later, needing a breath of air, he stepped out into the alley. He leaned against the freshly dark-blue-painted wall of the building and grumbled as he noticed a message that had been scrawled upon it, apparently during the night before, which invited any passerby to fuck himself. Reggie would get one of the café guys out here to paint it over. But for the moment, he wished to enjoy one more slice of the loaf, which he brought from the pocket of his apron. No butter. Delicious. The sun had come up and, the disrepute of the alley and its citizens aside, he enjoyed the light.

Looking to his left, he saw Amy. A meter maid, she had been a regular on the alley for some months, having been acknowledged by several of the residents during her daily route through The Tenderloin. She had told Reggie that there was no sense in treating these people badly. "They've just been unfortunate, so many of them," she had said. "You know, the drugs and all that." About forty, she was very thin, with a grey complexion that bespoke some sort of sickness and sadness in her own life. When Reggie engaged her in conversation, she seemed reticent to speak with him. She never precisely mentioned it, but he suspected a difficulty in her life, maybe even some kind of rough disaster that had disabled for her the possibility of plain enjoyment.

Reggie always served her coffee and a pastry, for free whenever she came into the bakery. She would be in uniform: the dark blue somberness of the police presence, but without all the weaponry. So…no handgun. No handcuffs. A badge, yes. Sitting at the café counter, she would finger the pastry, occasionally picking it up as though she did not know what it was and was wary of it. She paid more attention to the mug of coffee, but even this was given little credit for improving her morning. Amy thanked Reggie every time but could not get beyond the mono-syllabic responses that, for him, always distinguished her speech. Her cheeks sagged. She looked ill. Often, the pastry would be left behind, half-eaten, itself even more silent.

Until recently, when, Reggie noticed, she had begun wrapping the un-eaten portion in a neat napkin and taking it with her. It happened that her complexion was brightening as well.

Just now she was giving Abwan Jones a talk. Abwan was a ladder-tall black man, very friendly, who frequently backed up the singer whose recordings he was playing on his cellphone. (It still amazed Reggie that homeless people could afford cellphones…but so it was.) Just this morning it was Marvin Gaye, his *I heard it through the grapevine…*

"'Oo-ooh, I bet you wondered how I knew….'" Abwan's voice soared, interfering with Marvin's. Amy stood before him, facing him, her arms to her sides. The ticket book was in her left hand, and she was smiling. Abwan's eyes widened. "'Bout your plans to make me blue.'"

He seemed actually to be flirting with Amy, and so, was doubly enjoying the lyrics. He wore a long, dark brown overcoat, a pair of jeans raggedy around the cuffs, a San Francisco Giants T-shirt, and a scuffed, black fedora. He had told Reggie he was forty; but in terms of the lines in his face, he looked fifty or more, and his face also sagged with downturned unhappiness except for when he was listening to his music. The most distinguishing detail of Abwan's appearance was his cleanliness. Somewhere, he got a shower. Maybe every day.

"I'm a musician myself, man," he had once told Reggie. "I had a career of my own goin' for a while." When they had first met, early one morning at sun-up a few months earlier, Abwan had asked Reggie what he was doing on the alley.

"I work at the bakery."

"You the cook?"

"The baker, yes."

Abwan offered a conciliatory nod. "You know Amy, don't you? She gave me half of one of your cookies a while ago. Oatmeal."

"Did you like it?"

"Man, it was…what you call?…paradise!"

Abwan was not being intentionally rude to Amy just now. Reggie had noticed how they frequently spoke with one another. Abwan had a sense of humor, and he would kid Amy about her tickets. "Waste of time, Officer," he would say. "Nobody here payin' attention." He would turn and laugh, joined by some of the others sitting on the sidewalk nearby. Amy seemed to understand Abwan's gleefulness. She ventured another smile. She then advised a pair of tent dwellers that they couldn't set up in the metered parking place in which the tent just now lay flat and unfolded. If the tent were indeed still there in an hour, and especially if it were set up, she would write them a ticket.

"Why?" the homeless woman asked as she gestured toward the other tents.

"Quality of life issue," Amy said. Those tents were on the sidewalks, not in parking spaces. "And traffic safety." She folded the ticket book shut and placed it in a back pocket. "It's got to happen, Miss. We don't want anybody to get run over." Reggie knew that most of the tickets did get thrown away and suspected that Amy knew that as well. But he also knew how the tent indeed would be moved. Most probably, he thought, because the officer had suggested personally that it be so, and with kindness. The intimacy of that kind of order face to face had more weight than did a mere government-issue form.

Reggie took another bite from the coffee cake and leaned back against the wall. He glanced up the alley. Abwan and Amy were both looking the other way, their backs to Reggie. He noticed the exchange of a green something from the meter maid to Abwan, which he secreted into a pocket. Money. She turned from him toward the bakery, and Reggie was able to look away an instant before he would come into the meter maid's line of vision.

Later, Reggie was working the machine that made the super-thin croissant dough, and wondered how bakers had performed this task, those who had worked prior to the day on which this marvelous machine came to be. Josephine was working at a counter behind Reggie, her back to him, and as the machine wound up and down, back and forth spreading and flattening the dough thinner and thinner, he turned to address her.

"Amy was outside this morning," he said.

"I saw her." Josephine wore a white baker's smock that now was smudged with dough and other ingredients. This one was missing a button in front and loosened at the collar. Josephine had grown up in Bakersfield and was a big fan of Bakersfield's own, Merle Haggard. She had mentioned the singer during her job interview, and Reggie had asked her about him. Josephine said, "Listen, when you hear a lyric like ''Cause I'm always here at home 'til closin' time,' you know you've got somethin'." The day after he promoted her to assistant baker, Josephine brought her newlywed wife Lou Anne to the café. Unlike Josephine, whose hair was always a tight crewcut, Lou Anne's flowed from her in dark cobalt tresses. She also wore make-up, applied with care and taste, while Josephine made only an occasional uncaring nod to fashion. The two women clearly cared for each other, although Lou Anne had once admitted to Reggie that she didn't really listen much to country music. "I mean…." She glanced toward Josephine, taking her hand. "You know…."

"Who *do* you like?" Reggie said.

"Mozart!"

Both women laughed, embracing one another.

Reggie had described to Josephine how quickly Abwan had folded the bills from Amy and shoved them into his coat pocket.

"Amy buys drugs," Josephine said.

"Drugs!" Reggie lifted a hand to the side of his head. "She's a cop!" Chagrined, he rustled his hair.

"Yeah." Josephine grinned. "And Abwan is a nice man!" She shook her head with slow thoughtfulness. "So what?" Wiping her hands with a wet towel, she leaned back against the counter. "I mean, even I buy from him."

"You!"

Chagrined by her indiscretion, Josephine surrounded her hands in the towel once more, looking away. "Yeah…uh…a little apache now and then." She tightened her lips. "It never hurt anybody." She appeared to have taken fright, though, as though caught. "Does that bother you?"

"Uh…."

"You aren't going to fire me, are you, Reggie?"

Reggie frowned. "Of course not. You're responsible for that chocolate coffee cake." He saw how worried Josephine had quickly become. "Fire you!"

She lowered her head, staring at the floor. Her hands still wrung themselves within the towel.

"As long as, you know, you don't do it here," Reggie said. "And it doesn't affect what you do when you *are* here."

"I'm always on time, right?" Josephine grumbled.

"Yes, always."

"Always alert?"

"Every minute of the day!"

She turned back to her own counter. "That's the way I operate, Reggie. And that's a deal. I guarantee it."

Reggie demurred. He had told himself not to mind the drug sales in the alley. But in fact, he did mind. He didn't know what personally had caused all these people to be cast out onto the streets. But he suspected that the fentanyl so released them from their opinions of themselves that getting back indoors became more and more a foolishness for them. *Warmth! Comfort! Hey, man, we're high!*

He knew Josephine's guarantee was real, though, and he accepted it.

A few days later, Abwan's overcoat lay crumpled in an alley gutter, and the last anyone had seen of him was the evening before, when he had been accusing people of stealing his cell phone. One of the residents—Mel, who was white and bearded shaggy, an alcoholic Navy veteran who was more noted for the twice-daily bottle of Gallo red than for the filth of his USS Ronald Reagan baseball cap, who slept on the sidewalk outside the motorcycle repair garage up the alley—told of how Abwan had approached him and threatened him. "You know, the guy wouldn't listen!" Mel explained. "I mean, I like Abwan. But, man, he was bad yesterday!" Abwan had terrorized several others, and the conversation on the alley had to do with how that apache can make a monster out of you, man, even out of someone like Abwan Jones! His overcoat was all that was left of him the following morning.

Who seemed most affected by his disappearance was Amy. When she arrived later, her Go-For meter maid car parked at the head of the alley, she did not know of Abwan's disappearance. But once she heard of it from several residents, she came into the bakery.

"Have you seen him?"

Reggie and Josephine had brought her a plate with some of the new chocolate coffee cake, heated, a thick smudge of fresh butter, and a brimming mug of extra-hot coffee, just the way Amy liked it.

"No," Josephine said. "We were hoping you'd seen him."

"Nowhere." Amy chewed a moment on her lower lip, staring into the coffee. Her right hand on the counter was gathered into a gnarled-seeming fist. The feathery opening and shutting of the fingers indicated to Reggie the concern Amy had for Abwan. She played with the coffee cake and then, chagrined, turned away from it. Looking over her left shoulder, she appeared to be wishing that Reggie and Josephine weren't there staring at her. She was crestfallen. "I don't know where he is."

After a bit more clumsy back-and-forth, Reggie and Josephine excused themselves. "Got to get back to work," Reggie said. "If you see him…."

"Oh, I'll let you know," Amy said. She took a pen from the chest pocket of her uniform, asked Reggie for a piece of paper, and wrote on it. "This is my phone. A private number, so don't give it to anybody, please." She handed the note to Reggie. "And if *you* see him, call me."

As she left the counter, Amy gestured toward Josephine. She wished to speak with her alone, outside, and Josephine whispered to Reggie that she'd be right back. "Something's up," she whispered. She headed for the door into the alley. Coming back fifteen minutes later, her demeanor had changed.

"What's going on?" Reggie said.

"Can't talk."

"Come on, Josephine. What did Amy say?"

"No."

The initial resentment of Abwan's behavior among the alley dwellers changed to worry as, while the next days passed, he remained disappeared. Quiet—not the usual state of things on the alley—prevailed. Had Abwan been arrested? Was he dead? Reggie spoke a few more times with Amy, and with each conversation, her mood worsened. It was clear to Reggie that she feared the worst for Abwan, and Reggie supposed this was due to her knowledge that he was in the drug trade. Worker protection does not exist there, and Reggie feared that one day, Abwan's twisted, broken body would wash up on some sidewalk, so that his singing would be just as gone as his cell phone.

And then one day, he did show up. But this was not the Abwan that everyone knew. For one, he clearly had not had a recent shower, so that his appearance more closely resembled that of the other residents. A cloth jacket had replaced his overcoat, and the fedora was gone. A cloth bag hung from his right shoulder. All was soiled, especially the run-down Nike running shoes that were the norm for Abwan. He had been able to keep them washed, reminding everyone that if shoes like this were good enough for all those Nigerian distance runners, "they fast enough for Abwan Jones." The resultant laughter from the others ensured Abwan's self-confidence. But now the shoes were stained with mud and detritus, as were the socks. He seemed not to care.

Reggie heard about his return to the alley from Mel. Early one morning, there was a disturbance outside the bakery. The alley suffered from frequent moments of turmoil, and they usually were settled within a few minutes, with occasional woundings, but more frequently slowly diminishing outrage muddled with profanities. This confrontation, though, seemed to be going on for longer than usual, until finally Mel opened the side door and leaned into the kitchen.

"Reggie! Can you help us?"

Reggie tossed aside the shaped clod of ancient grains dough, one of dozens of loaves he and the crew were preparing for baking. When he arrived outside, he could see the levels of concern on the faces of many of the residents, those especially who were looking up toward the far end of the alley. Amy was leaning back against her meter maid car, and Abwan was standing directly before her, berating her. His right arm was extended, the hand closed into a fist except for its index finger, which was pointed directly at the meter maid's face.

"When you gonna leave me alone?"

"When you stop selling that apache…and especially when you stop *doing* the apache, Abwan."

"I do what I want."

"I know that. You're killing yourself."

"I am not. You're thinking too much, Amy. You don't know. How would you know?"

"Because I have eyes, Abwan. I can see."

Abwan turned away from her and hurried his hands into his pants pockets. He took a few paces away from Amy, turned and took a few back toward her, and turned again.

"Go ahead! Be the actor, Abwan." Amy was frightened, but it was clear that she would not be held back. "Academy Award!" She looked away a moment, and then turned toward him. "I quit, didn't I?"

Abwan shrugged, his back still turned to Amy. "Yeah, yeah…."

"Why can't you?"

"You shut up!"

"I did, Abwan!"

A confusion ran through the onlooking crowd. She quit?

"I did! So, what are you gonna do?"

Abwan turned away, finally silenced. He spotted Reggie, who was standing with the crowd of witnesses. Abwan spit onto the alley road surface, and fled past Amy and the meter maid car, toward Van Ness Avenue.

Reggie was joined by Josephine, and they approached Amy who, although shaken, even terrified, was able to retain her composure. She leaned against the car, her head held low. Josephine put her arms around Amy's shoulders. "Come on, we've got coffee for you."

"Leave me alone!"

"No, Amy. Forget the macho cop stuff. Just come in for a cup of coffee. We'll take care of you."

They passed back through the small crowd, and Amy actually got offerings of commiseration from a few of the homeless.

Abwan disappeared again, just as quickly, gone for five more days.

The coffee cake was as big a hit with the customers as Reggie had predicted. Whenever he received congratulations for it, he pointed out Josephine to the admirer. "It's all hers. Just following her directions, that's all I was doing." He knew how much the accolades pleased her, and they had begun work on a new project, a kind of super-dark chocolate cookie in a combination much like that of the coffee cake, although improved upon by, well, Josephine.

One morning, the new counter-guy came into the kitchen…Jim, who had joined the bakery a few days before and was already being noted for his kind handling of customers. He was just twenty years old, yet reminded Reggie of old photos he had seen of 1960s hippies. His very long dusty hair surged from beneath a Leon Russell-style cowboy hat, the combination brightened by a pair of rimless, round John Lennon sunglasses.

"There's an Indian guy out front. An old guy." Jim wore a blue cotton work shirt and a tie-dyed sleeveless vest. "He wants to talk to you, Reggie." He had attached a button to the vest that advised whoever was looking at it not to worry and to be happy.

Reggie glanced toward Josephine, who nodded. He wiped his hands clean. Coming out front, he saw the usual line at the cash register. A very dark man, clearly from the sub-continent—Indian, Pakistani or some such—sat at a table. He wore a white long sleeve shirt and dark slacks. About seventy-five, his still flourishing hair was straight and grey-black. He had not shaved in a few days, so that his whiskers looked like narrow snowflakes. His arms were crossed, and he appeared despondent, staring at his shoes. He wore thick glasses that sat at an angle upon his nose. Jim pointed him out.

"My name is Brajesh, Mr. Reggie." He offered his hand as Reggie sat down. "I am from the Hotel William down Geary Street there." He was a tall man with long arms. "One of our guests, he…." Brajesh tightened his lips and looked away. "A black man. He asked us to tell you…to tell you he is worried."

"Abwan?"

"Yes. Abwan." Brajesh folded his arms. "How did you know?" He looked down at the floor. "A Muslim name, no?"

"Maybe. I don't know."

"Yes, it is. I went to school with a boy named Abwan, before they moved to Pakistan." Brajesh shook his head. "We were friends. But our fathers were not."

"I see."

"A sadness."

"I imagine so."

"But this Abwan lives in The William, and *I* am worried about *him*." Brajesh reached into a shirt pocket and brought out a card. "I am the manager."

Reggie examined the card. "Is he alright?" Receiving no reply, he noticed how Brajesh's mouth resembled a worried-shut coin purse.

Brajesh searched for a reply. "No, he's not well."

"What's wrong?"

"He will not come out of his room."

"Does he say why?"

"No. And the first of the month came a few days ago."

"Yes?"

"And…no rent."

Reggie nodded. "I see."

"Abwan always pays his rent…the first of the month. Every month, right as…." With sudden intensity, Brajesh smiled. "What do the English say? Right as— "

"Right as rain."

"Yes." Brajesh sighed and looked to the floor. "But this month? No. I went to ask him about it this morning, and he would not come out."

"You talked with him?"

"Through the closed door, yes."

"What did he say?"

Brajesh's lips remained stiff. "I could not understand it." He glanced out the café window onto Taylor Street and shrugged. "It was…nuts."

"Nuts."

"Yes. No sense."

"He was raving?"

Brajesh's shoulders sunk even more. "What is that? That word. I've forgotten it. 'Raving?'"

"Shouting. Crazy."

"Yes. Very crazy."

Reggie excused himself and went to the kitchen, where he told Josephine what he knew. "I'll be back in a couple minutes." He put on his jacket.

"Should I call Amy?"

"No, not yet. Let me see what I can find out."

He followed Brajesh up the stairs from the hotel lobby. The lobby was itself just an extension of the hallway leading from the front door. That door was locked and protected by an iron gate outside. The lobby had a linoleum floor, a card table and two wooden chairs. Brajesh went behind the counter and brought out a key ring. The keys rattled and tingled as he searched for one particular one.

"Come along, then." He gestured toward a wooden stairway.

The hallway on the third floor was as lacking in decor as was the lobby. It was clean (as noted by Brajesh. "We have standards here, you know.") but featureless. As they approached the door to room 311, Brajesh held an index finger to his lips.

Reggie heard rough footsteps against a bare linoleum floor. Silence. An outcry.

"You hear?" Brajesh whispered. "It has been this way for two days. He won't come out."

"And before that, what was it like when he did come out."

"Confusion, Mr. Reggie! Anger."

"Did he attack anyone?"

"Abwan? No." Brajesh fingered the key. "But…sorrow." He shook his head with slow commiseration. "Sadness."

Reggie nodded and approached the door. "Abwan?" He knocked twice. But after a moment of silence, during which Abwan clearly was listening for more, the pacing returned. "Abwan, can we talk?" More pacing, and now a kind of loud muttering.

Reggie turned to Brajesh. "I see."

"What shall I do?" Worry remained on Brajesh's face. "Mr. Reggie?"

"Nothing, for the moment. But I know someone who knows Abwan. I'll ask her."

"Oh, thank you." Brajesh shook his head, a despondent-seeming scowl on his lips. "He is a nice bloke, this Abwan. I have told him about my school chum."

Reggie described for Josephine what he had witnessed. He needed advice. "Do we call Amy?"

There was no pause or hesitant worry. "Of course!"

"But she's a cop!"

"So?"

"We don't know what Abwan may have in his room."

Josephine nodded. She understood. She didn't care. "So what?"

"But, Josephine, she's got the power of arrest."

"And she's a woman, Reggie."

Reggie's teeth ground together. He grumbled.

"I've watched her with Abwan," Josephine said. "We talked about him." Her eyes widened with commiserative assurance. "Let me talk to her. She and I speak…you know, the…the same—"

"Same language."

"Yeah!" Josephine removed her baker's jacket. Underneath, she was wearing a T-shirt that showed the faces of Alexandra Ocasio Cortez and the rest of The Squad. "And I see that you have the capacity to, uh…" Looking down, she grinned. "…understand!" Reggie sensed that, although he may be getting it right in this particular instance, he would not get much else straight were he to sit in on intimate conversation about Abwan between Josephine and Amy. Reggie succumbed to Josephine's smile.

A few hours later, Josephine placed her phone in a rear pants pocket. "She says she wants to see him."

Reggie grimaced. "You don't mean she goes up to his room in uniform. Her badge big as can be? 'Let's roll, guys!'?"

"I don't know. But I think we better take her over there."

The next evening, Reggie and Josephine sat with Brajesh at the lobby table. Josephine had brought a box of pastries…a carton that held two croissants, two oatmeal cookies, a couple of slices of lemon bread, and two blueberry muffins. The bakery also carried a few lines of jams, and Reggie had suggested the dark blue multi-berry jam that came from a Marin County vendor, his personal favorite of all the confections they offered. The box itself was a visual smile: white cardboard printed with multiple shapes and doodads in black, with the name "Crusts of Bread & Such" spilling diagonally, as though hand-written with a black crayon, across the closed top.

Amy was late. "A lot of tickets today, I guess," Reggie worried.

"She'll be here," Josephine said.

"You talked to her?"

"This afternoon. Don't worry."

Brajesh, nervous, had been chewing on his thumb. "Our tenants do not like the police to be here."

"It's happened before?"

"Yes. Last year two of my guests…roommates…were arrested for heroin." He looked away, toward the running board below his office window. "Well, only one was arrested." He sighed. "We don't get much heroin here." He ran his tongue over his lips.

"How did those guys get in?"

"They seemed nice. They were dressed. Young. They paid up front." Brajesh sighed. "Gay boys."

"But heroin?"

"Yes. An overdose."

Reggie let out a breath.

"It was terrible, Mr. Reggie. So, the residents, they become nervous if a police chap shows up here."

"She's not a chap," Josephine said.

"Yes, Miss. I know. But still…."

"Don't worry. She told me about her plan. You'll see."

A few minutes later, the doorbell rang. The three looked toward Geary Street outside, and Brajesh stood and went to the office, to push the button that would allow the iron gate to open.

Amy surged into the lobby. Not in uniform. Reggie's eyes widened. He felt they might make a noise doing so. "Amy!"

She was dressed in black, a silk dress, the top half embroidered with light grey sensuous roses. The dress's skirt was expanded about the lower quarter with extra flourishes of silk embroidery. Her shoes, which resembled dance pumps, revealed lovely toes, their nails colored perhaps that very day, unlike what you would expect were you to see her only in her police officer boots. She had a small grey leather bag with a silver chain, and light, finessed eye makeup.

"How do I look, Josephine?"

Josephine sighed. She was flustered with surprise. "Just…well, fine!"

"You're sure."

"Believe me, I…I…."

"Where is he?"

They made their way up to Room 311. Josephine had handed Amy the box of pastries and described what was inside. As they approached the door, they heard Abwan's ravings. They were louder now than they had been with Reggie's visit the day before and less icily crazy. More spectral.

Amy looked to Josephine and Reggie for assurance and cradled the box of pastries with her left arm. She took in a breath as she tried gathering herself. Josephine patted her on the shoulder and motioned to the others to step away from the door…indeed to retreat down the hallway toward the stairs. Once she was alone, Amy knocked on the door.

"Abwan?"

The raving ceased.

"It's me, Amy. Will you let me in?"

Silence changed the atmosphere in the hallway, as did, after a moment, the voice behind the door.

"Amy?"

"Yes, it's me."

"Who sent you?"

"Nobody. I just came over to see you."

More silence.

"Please, Abwan?"

The door opened. All Reggie could see was a hand and a bare forearm reaching out into the hallway. Amy took the hand into hers and entered the room.

There was no noise the entire night. Brajesh kept an eye on things until midnight, and was replaced by Reggie, who told Josephine when she arrived at three o'clock that he would be at the bakery. "Call me if anything happens."

Reggie, working with the bakery crew, received no phone call from Josephine. No sense of alarm. Nothing, except for an email that said there was no raving from Abwan. Finally, she came into the kitchen at 7:30.

"Brajesh is there. He'll call us if anything comes up. But mostly I'm concerned for Amy. There hasn't been any noise at all from Abwan's room. It just stopped, the moment she went in. He hasn't…. You know, hasn't…."

The side door to the kitchen opened, and Brajesh walked in. He was nervous.

"You had better come," he said. Distracted, he turned back to the door, and was followed with hurried anxiety by Reggie and Josephine.

Josephine approached the door. The hallway was quiet, except for their careful footsteps. When they gathered outside Room 311, the only thing to be heard was breathing from each other. Josephine glanced toward the others, and then turned to the door and knocked.

For a moment, there was no sound. Then some footsteps, quiet, unhurried.

"Who is it?"

"Amy, it's me. Josephine."

"Oh!"

"Are you okay?"

"I'm fine."

"You're sure?"

"Yes."

They heard a few more steps back and forth, and some whisperings. Then the door latch being loosened and the turning of the doorknob.

Amy, dressed as she had been the evening before, refreshed and smiling, came out, closing the door quietly behind her.

Reggie had not known what to expect. Her appearance the night before had shocked him, so that he now realized she had a far more complicated life than being just a cop. Her manner had been clarified. She had confidence in what she knew, and in what to do. Abwan's retreat into quiet had come in the same moment he had opened the door of his room to her.

"He just needed some happiness, Josephine," Amy said. The two women embraced.

Josephine took Amy's hands into hers and examined them. "No. He needed you." Her voice softened the moment so successfully that Reggie's breathing itself eased.

Amy adjusted her hair. "Just leave him alone for now. He's asleep."

They descended the stairway and gathered in the lobby. The sidewalk outside was deserted. Sunlight emblazoned the street.

"Will he come out again?" Reggie said.

Amy looked away, out the front window of the hotel. Mel was walking past. Bent over slightly, he held his customary backpack, blotched with stain like so many of the tents on the alley, with his right hand, securing it to his back as he stumbled. Righting himself, he let out an angry vulgarity and proceeded on.

"No."

Reggie looked to Josephine, who was also awaiting more explanation.

"Well…yes," Amy said. She took Josephine's hand. "He's…." With her free hand, Amy fiddled with the latch of her purse. "He's…."

Reggie and Josephine remained quiet. Brajesh as well.

"He's coming with me."

"You mean…" Reggie's jaw tightened. "To jail?"

Amy inhaled and took Josephine's hand more firmly. "No, Reggie." She looked over her shoulder, up the stairs. "No."

Terence Clarke lives in San Francisco.